William E. Decrow

Yale and the City of Elms

Third Edition

William E. Decrow

Yale and the City of Elms
Third Edition

ISBN/EAN: 9783337406127

Printed in Europe, USA, Canada, Australia, Japan

Cover: Foto ©Andreas Hilbeck / pixelio.de

More available books at **www.hansebooks.com**

YALE

AND

"THE CITY OF ELMS"

BY W. E. DECROW

Illustrated with Heliotypes

OF ALL THE PRINCIPAL COLLEGE BUILDINGS, A PLAN OF THE COLLEGE
GROUNDS, AND A MAP OF THE CITY OF NEW HAVEN

THIRD EDITION

Boston
W. E. DECROW, 238 WASHINGTON STREET
1885

INTRODUCTION.

"YALE and the 'City of Elms,'" is intended chiefly as a guide to the visitor to Yale College, yet containing sufficient information concerning the City of New Haven to enable him to at once seek out the principal points of interest in and about the home of the College, and learn a few of the more important facts regarding the many noteworthy features of the city.

The book contains, it is hoped, so much of the history of each department of the University as is necessary to convey to the reader a fair idea of the institution and its purposes, at the same time not exceeding the bounds of a hand-book to accompany the visitor and give him a description of the various buildings and other objects of interest in his walk through the college grounds and the city.

By referring to the plan of the grounds and buildings published in the first part of the work, the visitor will have no difficulty whatever in finding the objects mentioned, and will notice that, in a general way, the buildings are described according to location, so that, by following the order of the book, all the buildings and objects of interest may be seen and visited with the least possible amount of travel.

The heliotype illustrations, which with one or two exceptions were made from negatives taken specially for "Yale and the 'City of

Elms'" by Mr. James Notman of Boston, will perhaps serve, among other purposes, that of aiding the friends of Yale who cannot personally visit New Haven to take a pleasant imaginary stroll through the grounds and buildings of the College and the city.

The sources of information in book form from which the facts contained in "Yale and the 'City of Elms'" have been derived were principally that grand work commonly known as the "Yale Book," and the mirror of student life entitled "Four Years at Yale." The writer, who feels indebted to various gentlemen for valuable assistance, is under especially great obligations to Professor F. B. Dexter for almost indispensable aid; to Mr. Thomas R. Trowbridge, Jr., of the New Haven Colony Historical Society, for numerous facts concerning the city; and to Professor A. W. Phillips for very important help.

INDEX.

ILLUSTRATIONS.

HELIOTYPES.

PLATES AND MAPS.

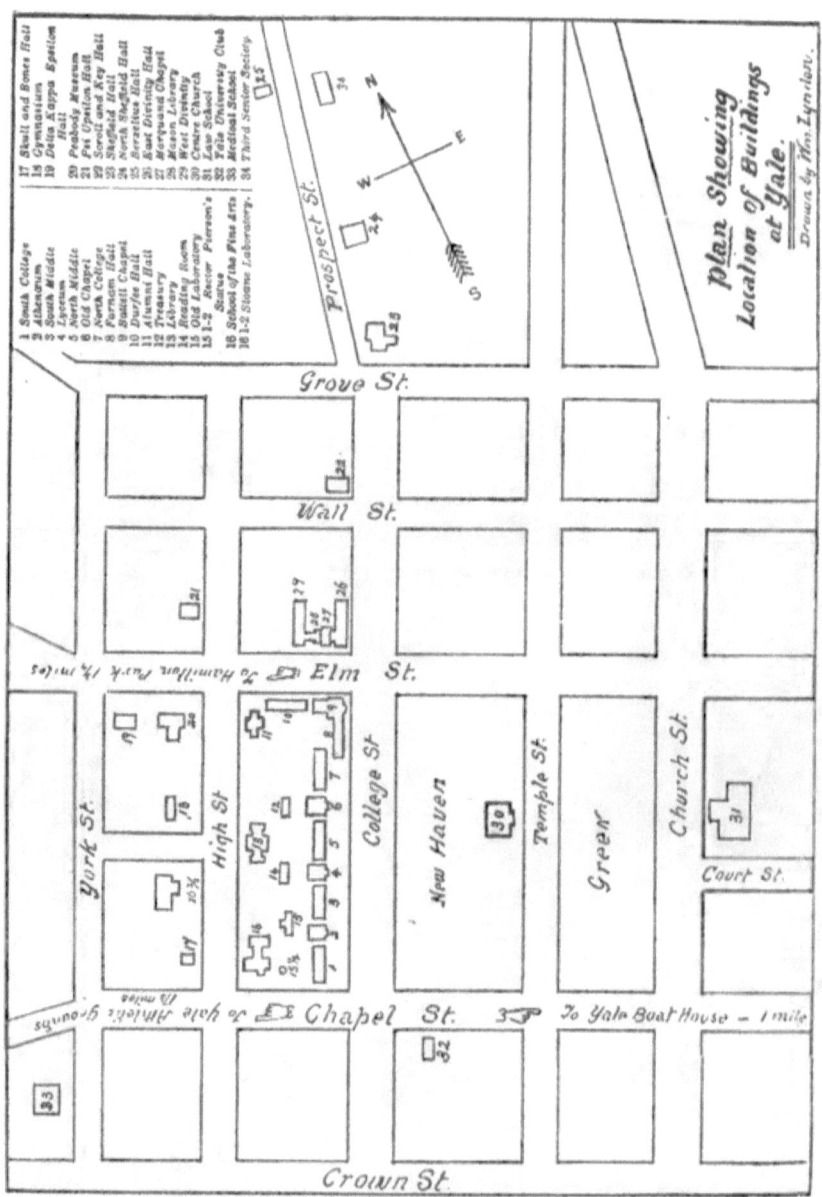

Plan Showing
Location of Buildings
at Yale.

Drawn by Wm. Lyman.

1 South College
2 Atheneum
3 South Middle
4 Speram
5 North College
6 Old Chapel
7 North College
8 Farnam Hall
9 Battell Chapel
10 Durfee Hall
11 Alumni Hall
12 Treasury
13 Library
14 Reading Room
15 1-2 Old Laboratory
    Statue
16 Rector Pierson's
17 School of the Fine Arts
18 1-2 Sloane Laboratory.

17 Skull and Bones Hall
18 Gymnasium
19 Delta Kappa Epsilon
    Hall
20 Peabody Museum
21 Psi Upsilon Hall
22 Scroll and Key Hall
23 Sheffield Hall
24 North Sheffield Hall
25 Berzelius Hall
26 East Sheffield Hall
27 East Divinity Hall
28 Marquand Chapel
29 West Divinity
30 Centre Church
31 West Church
32 Law School
33 Yale University Club
34 Medical School
34 Third Senior Society

HISTORICAL SKETCH.

YALE COLLEGE, situated in the beautiful city of New Haven, Connecticut, had its origin away back in the very beginning of the eighteenth century, nearly two hundred years ago. From the moment of the settlement of New Haven colony, in 1638, the leading spirit among the settlers, John Davenport, had determined upon the organization of a college, and less than ten years after that time, a lot of land had been set aside at New Haven and called " college land." But various difficulties presented themselves, so that Davenport died without witnessing the fruition of his purpose. The project was never abandoned, however, and in 1664 a collegiate school, called Hopkins Grammar School, in honor of its benefactor, Governor Hopkins of Connecticut, was successfully organized. The fact that the instruction given was not up to the requirements of a college course led ten ministers of the colony of Connecticut to organize themselves into a society for the establishment of a collegiate school. In the fall of the year 1700 or 1701 they met at Branford, and each laid on the table at the place of meeting, a few volumes, saying, " I give these books for founding a college in this colony." This act is generally looked upon as the beginning of Yale College. From so humble an origin has sprung the powerful Yale University of to-day.

For a time the college was located at Saybrook, Connecticut, under Rev. Abraham Pierson, who was chosen Rector. Jacob Hemingway, who entered in March, 1702, was the first student. After wandering about from town to town, to accommodate itself to the residences of the various officials, the college at last became permanently located at

New Haven. Much opposition was manifested to its removal to that place; in fact, force had to be used in transferring the library from Saybrook to its new home, and one hundred and sixty volumes were lost in the scuffles which occurred on the journey.

The first public Commencement of the college at New Haven occurred in 1718. Those who had seceded on the removal of the college to that place held a rival Commencement at Wethersfield, but a reconciliation was brought about, and all the factions at length united heartily in support of the college in its new location.

In 1717 the first college building was erected, about which time Governor Elihu Yale, of London, made to the institution several valuable gifts, including "books, the portrait and the arms of King George, and £200 sterling worth of English goods," out of gratitude for which, the trustees named the new building Yale College. Governor Yale was born in New England, educated in England, and became Governor of Fort St. George, now Madras. The college possesses an original full-length portrait of its great benefactor. His epitaph in the churchyard at Wrexham, in Wales, where Governor Yale was buried, contains the following lines:

> " Born in America, in Europe bred,
>   In Afric travelled and in Asia wed,
>   Where long he lived and thrived; at London dead.
>   Much good, some ill he did; so hope's all even,
>   And that his Soul through Mercy's gone to Heaven."

In 1722 the college was shaken to its foundations by the apostacy of its Rector, Rev. Timothy Cutler, who became a communicant of the Church of England; and again in President Clap's term of office, from 1739 to 1766, much ill-feeling was created in and against the college on account of the stand taken by the authorities toward the great revival preacher, Whitefield, and his followers. Its sorest trial came during the American Revolution, however. Owing to the impossibility of procuring provisions in New Haven at this time, the Freshmen were removed to Farmington, and the Juniors and Sophomores to Glastonbury, the Seniors alone remaining in New Haven. Yale's record during that period is a proud one. A company of its students was reviewed and drilled on the Green at New Haven by General Washington while on his way to take command of the American forces about Boston; and it may be noted that this was the first military organization to receive orders from Washington after his appointment as Commander-in-Chief of the American forces. At the battle of Bunker Hill, Yale men stood shoulder to shoulder with their countrymen to repel the assaults of the invader, and scarcely a battle occurred during the War for Independence in which Yale was not represented. It was a Yale man, Captain Nathan Hale, of the class of 1773, who, having been selected by Washington as the most competent person in the entire American army to undertake the exceedingly hazardous enterprise of going within the British camp on Long Island as a spy, and having been captured (after fully accomplishing his mission), and condemned to die, in his last words exclaimed, "I regret that I have only one life to give for my country!"

In July, 1779, New Haven was taken, college buildings and all, by the British; not, however, until the red-coats had met with a vigorous resistance from students and citizens. On account of the war, no public Commencements were held between 1777 and 1781.

During President Stiles's administration of the college, beginning in 1777 and ending in 1795, the ill-feeling generated during the presidency of Clap disappeared, and a reconciliation came about, when, in return for a grant of money to the college, the Governor, Lieutenant Governor and six Senators of the State of Connecticut became members of the college corporation. Since that time Yale has had few, if any, drawbacks worthy of mention. Crippled by poverty for the first 130 years of its existence, it pressed bravely forward, ever increasing in excellence of education and in number of students, and never failing for a moment to retain its position in the very first rank of American colleges. Fifty years ago its first large endowment, of $100,000, was undertaken; "and it is worthy of notice, as one of the great results of that solid financial advance which began in 1831, that the aggregate of its academical graduates for the half-century now ending largely surpasses that of any other college in America."

The governing board at Yale, termed the Corporation, as at present constituted, consists of eighteen persons, viz.: the Governor and the Lieutenant Governor of the State of Connecticut, ten Congregational clergymen, who elect their own successors, and six gentlemen, elected one each year for a term of six years, by the graduates of five years' standing and upwards. The corporation meets at least once in each year, but a committee of its members, called the Prudential Committee, assembles as often as circumstances require. The arrangement of details for the government and maintenance of the institution is left, however, almost entirely to the president and to the faculties of the various departments.

At a meeting of the corporation in 1872, it was resolved that Yale had, by the successful establishment of the various departments, attained the form of a University, and that it be recognized as comprising the four departments of which a University is commonly understood to consist, viz.: the Departments of Theology, of Law, of Medicine, and of Philosophy and the Arts. Under the last-named department are included, the Courses for Graduate Instruction, the Undergraduate Academical Department, the Undergraduate Section of the Sheffield Scientific School, and the School of the Fine Arts — each having a distinct organization. The legal designation remains as before the organization into a University, "The President and Fellows of Yale College in New Haven."

The growth of Yale has been steady and rapid, both in number of students and in wealth. Fifteen years ago the number of students in the entire University was 682; for several years past the number has at no time been below 1,000; and lately has exceeded that figure. Fifteen years ago the number of officers of government and instruction was forty-nine; now, it exceeds twice that. As to material wealth, Yale is richer to-day by three millions of dollars, than she was a decade and a half ago, the value of all the property owned by the University being in 1884 perhaps seven millions of dollars. Much of this is in land and buildings.

Since its organization Yale College has conferred more than twelve thousand degrees, over nine thousand of which have been given to graduates of the Academical Department. Adding to the whole number of degrees conferred the number of those who graduated from the Law and the Theological Departments before degrees were conferred upon those who had completed the courses in law and theology, the total number of Yale graduates exceeds sixteen thousand; — an aggregate considerably greater than the number of graduates of any other college in the United States. The list includes the names of many of the most distinguished men of modern times, among whom may be mentioned both the great lexicographers, Webster and Worcester; the distinguished jurists, Grimke, Mason, and Calhoun; Morse, the inventor of the telegraph; Eli Whitney, inventor of the cotton-gin; Silliman, the greatest scientist of his generation; the learned Hadley, and the accurate thinker Chauvenet. Chief-Justice Waite and ex-Justice Strong, of the United States Supreme Court, Senator Dawes of Massachusetts, Hon. William M. Evarts, ex-Governor Samuel J. Tilden, and ex-Attorneys General Taft and Pierrepont are all graduates of Yale.

Yale has often been called the " Mother of Colleges," on account of her preponderating influence in the establishment of other institutions of learning. She has furnished the first president for very many American colleges, including Princeton, Columbia, Dartmouth, Williams, Georgia University, Hamilton, Kenyon, Illinois, Wabash, University of Missouri, University of Mississippi, University of Wisconsin, Beloit, College of Mississippi, Chicago University, California University, Cornell University and Johns-Hopkins University. She has furnished two presidents each to Middlebury, Rutgers, Illinois, Hampden-Sidney, Vermont University, Wisconsin University, Washington University, University of California, University of Georgia and

University of Mississippi; **and three** each to Columbia, Princeton **and Western Reserve;** also one each to several other colleges and universities, including **Trinity, College of South Carolina,** College of East Tennessee, **Iowa University and** the University **of** Kentucky. The **result has** been that a great majority **of the more** prominent American colleges have been, and are conducted on essentially the **Yale system, though the details** vary more or **less in** all of them. **At this point it** may not be inappropriate to give **a** brief statement of the **policy** pursued **by** this " Mother of Colleges," which can best **be done by** taking the following extract from **an official** report made by President Porter to the Society of the Alumni of **Yale,** in June, 1881 :

· " The institution has had a definite policy to which it has adhered with **a good** degree of consistency. **It has employed little active agency to** solicit funds. It has proposed **no royal or** easy paths to learning or intellectual **power.** It has carefully refrained from odious comparisons to the disadvantage of sister institutions. **It has avoided appeals to** the indolence or **the** undue self-reliance **which are characteristic of young men. On the** other hand, if the testimony **of those who have known its inmost spirit** and its animating **forces is** worth anything, it has not been too bigoted to learn nor too conceited to improve. **Its windows are** open in every direction, towards the rising as **truly as** towards the setting **sun, and it is ever ready to** welcome new **truth** from any quarter, and **to** try new methods, by whomsoever they **are** suggested, if they are **recommended** to our judgment or are enforced by experience. **But it believes in the past as** well as in **the** future, holding **it to be eminently** becoming in those who have received the **torch** of knowledge from those who have **gone before them, to despise** none of the wisdom which **the past has inspired or confirmed."**

As **an evidence of the** conservatism **thus expressed, it may be stated that during Yale's** almost two centuries **of existence,** but eleven **persons have filled the office of President of the college.** President **Day served from 1817 till 1846 — a period of** twenty-nine years. The Presidents have been : **Abraham Pierson** (1701–1707), Samuel Andrew

(1707–1719), Timothy Cutler (1719–1722), Elisha Williams (1725–1739), Thomas Clap (1739–1766), Naphtali Daggett (1766–1777), Ezra Stiles (1777–1795), Timothy Dwight (1795–1817), Jeremiah Day (1817–1846), Theodore D. Woolsey (1846–1871). The present incumbent, Rev. Noah Porter, D.D., LL.D., was chosen in 1871.

As is very well known, Yale is the most cosmopolitan of all American colleges — a characteristic for which it has been distinguished during more than a century and a half. It has drawn and continues to draw its students from all parts of the world. As a result, its graduates are found everywhere — particularly, in the United States, in New York, the West and the South. There is something in the Yale system which binds its students, drawn from so many different countries and States, with strong ties of class-friendship, this friendship tending to place all its students on terms of almost perfect equality. The man of wealth and the one who "works his way through," are held in equal esteem by all connected with the University. A manly, straightforward, capable student is sure to receive honor and respect, from both the authorities and his fellows, without regard to factitious distinctions of any sort whatever; and best of all, the friendly ties formed during the course are not broken at graduation, but manifest themselves ever through life in the form of class-feeling and loyalty to "Dear Old Yale." Between students and faculty, too, an excellent understanding prevails; and it is indeed a rare occurrence when any serious difficulty takes place. Though the students do not always see a given subject in the same light that it is seen by the corporation and the faculty, they nevertheless always quietly submit, never for an instant doubting the motive. So of the elements known as "Old Yale" and "Young Yale." However much their views may differ as to the policy to be pursued, each believes heartily in the sincerity of the other's efforts for the good of

"The Old — the New — the same dear Yale."

As would naturally be expected from its leading position, the amount of study necessary to enable one to pass the entrance examinations at Yale, and the amount of study required to maintain one's position in his class, is at least equal to that of any other American University. In fact, many are inclined to think that in order to pass through the course, more real, solid, steady work is required than at any other. This is in no sense a disadvantage, however, as the work is so laid out that the faithful student is able to accomplish it without injury to mind or body, and cannot fail to be the gainer.

Affording, as Yale does, so excellent and so entirely unexcelled an opportunity for a thorough education of the highest grade, the necessary annual expenses for a student are decidedly moderate, as will be seen by the following estimate, which includes everything but wearing apparel, travelling, and board in vacations: —

Treasurer's bill (according to location of room), from	$160 to	$220
Board, 37 weeks, ... "	130 to	220
Fuel, lights, and washing, . . . "	30 to	60
Use of text-books and furniture, . . "	30 to	60
Total, . . .	$350	$560

This is providing, of course, that the student is able to pay all necessary bills without aid. But if he cannot command this amount, he is at liberty to apply for a portion of the funds provided for such cases, always on the condition, however, that he be a worthy, faithful student. There are numerous ways in which he may earn money, so that it may safely be said that no deserving student is ever obliged to leave Yale for want of funds.

As it may prove of interest to the visitor to know what is required for admission to the college, the following schedule is given, showing the books and subjects in which all candidates for admission to the Freshman class of the Academical Department or college proper, are examined. The requirements for admission to the various other departments are given in their appropriate places elsewhere in this book: —

Latin Grammar.

Cæsar — Gallic War, Books I-III.

Cicero — Orations against Catiline and for Archias.

Virgil — Bucolics, and first six books of the Æneid, including Prosody.

Ovid — Metamorphoses, translation at sight.

The translation, at sight, of passages from prose Latin.

The translation into Latin of a connected passage of English prose.

Roman History.

Greek Grammar — with translation of English into Greek.

Xenophon — Anabasis, three books.

Homer — Iliad, two books, with Prosody.

The translation, at sight, of passages from Cicero or Cæsar.

Greek History.

French or German so far as to translate at sight easy prose, the candidate being in each case at liberty to decide for himself in which of the two languages he shall be examined.

Higher Arithmetic — including the metric system of weights and measures.

Algebra — so much as is included in Loomis's Treatise, up to the chapter on Logarithms.

Geometry — Euclid, book first, and the first 33 exercises thereon in Todhunter's edition; or, the first four books in other Geometries, with the above exercises.

Candidates who present themselves at the June examinations, may pass in part of the studies required; they must pass in at least seven of the subjects required, in order to receive any certificate; they may offer any subjects except reading Greek and Latin at sight. To save expense to candidates, special examinations are held at Chicago, Cincinnati and San Francisco each year.

The Academical Department.

A Jaunt Through the Grounds.— The visitor, having read the preceding sketch of the history of Yale, is prepared to take a jaunt through the College grounds for the purpose of examining the various halls, libraries, chapels and other objects of interest connected with the University. By referring to the printed plan, all difficulty in finding the different objects described will disappear. The most satisfactory starting-point will be the corner of Chapel and College streets, inasmuch as, passing through the gate on Chapel Street near College, the visitor at once comes upon the "Old Brick Row," for many years the principal buildings connected with the College.

The Campus.— But first the visitor will observe the remarkable beauty of the campus, or that portion of the University grounds bounded by Chapel, High, Elm, and College streets. Generations ago rows of elms were planted there, and are now grown up into noble shade-trees, beneath whose wide-spreading branches thousands of students have wended their way, and in whose shade many of America's most learned scholars, distinguished statesmen, and eminent teachers received the education which aided them to become the great public benefactors that they were. Webster and Worcester, of dictionary fame; Hadley, the great philologist; Silliman, the scientist; Morse, the inventor of the telegraph; Edwards, Hopkins, Emmons, Dwight, and Taylor, the eminent theologians; the distinguished writers

SOUTH.
(Page 11.)

Pierpont, Hillhouse, Cooper, Percival, Willis, Bushnell, Judd, Bristed, Mitchell, Winthrop and Stedman; the renowned jurists and barristers Grimke, Mason, Kent and Calhoun, and hosts of others scarcely less noted have been frequenters of the elm-clad campus at Yale. When Noah Webster (class of 1778) was in college, the campus embraced but a comparatively small portion of the ground now occupied by the Academical Department, extending north from Chapel Street only a short distance beyond the structure to-day known as South Middle, and but a few feet west of the present Old Laboratory. Additions have from time to time been made, however, until the campus now extends nearly nine hundred feet on College and High streets, and nearly five hundred feet on Chapel and Elm streets, embracing an entire double square. The campus has witnessed many jolly and exciting times among the students,—occasions which none but collegians can appreciate. Not infrequently the campus is lighted up at night by huge bonfires, for which the sophomores are generally responsible, though often the graduating class has, on Commencement night, a great fire in front of South College, when old chairs, dilapidated tables, the contents of kerosene cans, etc., are heaped together in one great mass and allowed to burn in honor of the occasion. The shadows cast by the noble old elms on these occasions lend a weirdness and grandeur to the scene, at once attractive, suggestive, and impressive.

But, to the buildings. Standing within an arm's length of Chapel Street, and about one hundred and thirty feet west of College Street, in "The Old Brick Row" is the venerable edifice designated: —

SOUTH COLLEGE. — South College, the most southerly building, as its name indicates, in this "Old Brick Row," is, next to South Middle, the oldest dormitory on the grounds, having been erected in 1793-4. The funds, some $13,000, were furnished by the State of Connecticut, with the condition that "the Governor, Lieutenant-Governor, and six senior Senators of the State, for the time being, should ever after be, by virtue of their offices, Trustees or Fellows of the College, and should, with the President and other Fellows, constitute the corporation, and enjoy the same powers and privileges as if they had been named in the charter." The condition was accepted, and South College was the immediate result. It is a plain brick building, one hundred feet long by forty wide, and originally contained thirty-two studies with two bed-rooms each. "In commemoration of the State's munificence and of the union in the corporation of ecclesiastics and civilians" the build-ing was named Union Hall, but has long since dropped that title and is now known officially and unofficially as "South." Like all the other dormitories it has been the scene of many a stirring event; but the most exciting of all occurred in 1855, when, in the great riot of that year between the students and the young men of the town, the stu-dents, pursued by hundreds of enraged townspeople, retired within the walls of South, barricaded the doors and prepared to fight to the death. A large loaded cannon was dragged to the spot by the towns-people, directed point-blank at the devoted building, and, so the story goes, had the gun not been spiked by a friendly hand, would have been discharged at the venerable pile. Finally, the reading of the riot act, and a display of military, coupled with a heavy rain, dispersed the mob, and South was thus saved, perhaps, from destruction. South College has always been a great favorite with the students, especially seniors, for various reasons, not the least important of which is its proximity to "The Fence." Of late its rooms in odd years are nearly all filled with seniors, and in even years by juniors. Among other con-veniences, or rather luxuries, many of its rooms, which are very cosey, contain open fire-places. Like all other buildings in the College it is supplied with gas and water. Among the distinguished persons who have roomed in South are Hons. Mason Brown (room 25), and Garnet Duncan (room 30), of Kentucky; Hon. Christopher Morgan (room 14), "Prince" John Van Buren (room 16), Rev. Dr. Budington (room 16), and Charles Astor Bristed (room 1), of New York; Professors James D. Dana (room 16), and Thomas A. Thacher (room 7), of New Haven; and Bishop Kip (room 7), of California.

ATHENÆUM.—The Athenæum, the second building north from Chapel Street in the "Old Brick Row," was originally built for a chapel, and was the first building erected specially for that purpose in the College grounds. By a vote of the corporation in 1760 it was decided that the new building should be of brick, fifty feet long and forty wide, with a library over it. It was completed in 1763, and was at once made use of, as well for exercises in oratory as in religion. In 1803, after the removal of the library to the Lyceum, then new, the upper story of the chapel was "thrown into three apartments: one for a philosophical room, another for an apparatus room, and a third for a museum." In 1824 the building ceased to be used for religious exercises, a new edifice, now known as Old Chapel, having been erected for that purpose. The structure then took the name Athenæum, which it now bears. The lower portion from that time onward was used for recitation rooms, and the upper portion for the society libraries. Formerly a spire surmounted the Athenæum, but this was taken down in 1829 and "replaced by an octagonal tower, built in imitation of the Tower of the Winds in Athens and fitted up for an observatory and to receive a telescope which had been presented to the College by Mr. Sheldon Clark. This telescope was a refractor of ten feet focal length, made by Dollond, of London, and is supposed to have been the best telescope at that time in America." In 1870 the tower was surmounted by a revolving cylindrical dome, and the Clark telescope occupies a position in it, though it is little used, comparatively, owing to better facilities now afforded in other departments of the University. Also in 1870, the whole interior of the Athenæum was rebuilt, and now contains four large recitation rooms for the freshman class. The original cost of the Athenæum was about $4,000. Visitors desirous of going up into the tower for a bird's-eye view of the College and its surroundings will find no difficulty in obtaining a key if application be made at the office of the college inspector, room number 2, Treasury, Mr. Frank E. Hotchkiss, the inspector, taking great pleasure in affording every possible courtesy to visitors.

SOUTH MIDDLE. — South Middle, built in 1750, is distinguished from the fact that it is the oldest building now standing in the entire University. In 1748 the number of students had so greatly increased that a new dormitory became an absolute necessity. To raise the required funds the General Assembly of the colony ordered that a lottery be held, and a board of directors was appointed for that purpose. This expedient proved successful, and the building was at once erected, though not entirely completed until several years later. When finished "it was the most elegant and the best building in the colony." It is of brick, with sandstone trimmings, is one hundred and five feet long and forty feet in breadth, and was originally three stories high, with a "French" or "gambrel" roof. This gambrel roof was removed in 1797, and a full story, covered with the present roof, put on. South Middle contained, after the extra story had been added, thirty-two studies, suitable for two students each. What was at one time a famous institution in the College, occupied the southeast corner room, ground floor, and was called the buttery. It was presided over by an officer called the butler, who had the exclusive right to sell, on the college grounds, such articles as "cider, metheglin, strong beer to the amount of not more than ten barrels annually (afterward increased to twenty), loaf sugar, pipes, tobacco, and such other necessaries of scholars as were not furnished in the commons hall." On the books of the butler no less a person than President Stiles is charged with such articles as cider, walnuts, pipes, porter, bottles of ale, biscuit and raisins. The buttery was abolished in 1817, after a long existence, having been established shortly after the building was completed. For many years the college bookseller occupied a room in South Middle, with his wares, but was finally obliged to withdraw a few years ago, and the rooms on the first floor, between the two entries, were thrown into one large room, which served as a reading-room until in 1877 that valuable institution was removed to its present quarters in the Philosophical Building.

The rooms in South Middle hall were, until 1883, for years occupied exclusively by sophomores, except the few rooms reserved for members of the faculty, and have doubtless witnessed within their walls more ludicrousness and the concocting of more well-laid schemes of mischief than all other rooms in College together. Though the building is so old and its timbers so warped that it is almost like taking an ocean voyage to walk some of the floors, or go down the flights of stairs, yet the average sophomore would prefer it, with its glorious associations, to the finest palace in America; and hundreds of dollars have been paid every year (until in 1881 the faculty put a stop to the practice) for the choice of a room there. Old graduates on the verge of the grave look back with glee to the uproarious fun they made a part of while inmates of South Middle, and laugh until tears run down their cheeks, in recollection of the various tricks and pranks planned within its walls.

LYCEUM.—The Lyceum, standing next north of South Middle in the "Old Brick Row," was completed in 1804 at a cost of perhaps $6,000. It is of brick, three stories high, 56 feet long, and 44 feet wide, with a tower in front surmounted by a cupola. The third floor was originally used for the library, while the first and second floors were partitioned off into recitation rooms. With the exception that the library has long since been removed, the rooms are used for about the same purposes now as when first built, viz., for recitations. The large room in the rear, on the first floor, known as the President's old lecture-room, is used by the students as a place in which to hold their class meetings and meetings for the election of officers for the various athletic organizations. Formerly the chemical laboratory was located in the basement of the Lyceum. Hanging in the cupola is the college bell, which has for generation after generation called the students to religious and literary exercises, and continues so to do; and though the college rules do not provide for such occasions, the same old bell has pealed out time and again the glad notes of victory in athletic contests with other colleges — victories which were doubly prized from the fact of the great skill and excellence of the opponents from whom they were won. Previous to the completion of Battell Chapel the college clock occupied a position in the tower of Lyceum, and its old, time-worn wooden dials may be seen there yet. In the last days of its activity this instrument went in a fearful and wonderful way, and, like Paddy's timepiece, kept more time than any other clock in town.

NORTH MIDDLE. — North Middle College, built in 1803, and standing next north of Lyceum, is similar in general appearance to the other dormitories in the "Old Brick Row," which, by the way, from their plainness and uniformity, have sometimes been called " the factories." It is 106 feet long by 40 feet wide, is four stories high, and originally accommodated about 96 students. It is heated by steam, is provided with gas and water, and on the whole is a very comfortable dormitory, though the condition of the floors, window-caps, etc., indicates that it was not as well built as some of its neighbors. Each room contains, against the wall next the sleeping-rooms, a large closet with double doors. It was intended that a bed should be placed in this closet, capable of being lowered to the floor at night to accommodate an occupant, so that each study could provide sleeping accommodations for three persons. These closets are now used for wardrobes, merely. Until North College was built, North Middle was the most popular dormitory in the row, and was consequently occupied by seniors. After 1821 the seniors deserted it for the then new North College, and North Middle became, what it continues to be, the headquarters, in this set of buildings, for the juniors, though the upper story is reserved for freshmen. Unlike South Middle and South, this dormitory has led a very quiet, uneventful life, with scarcely a ripple of excitement of any kind, though hundreds of graduates doubtless look back with pleasure upon many a happy evening passed in old North Middle. Among the distinguished persons who have occupied rooms within its walls, are Rev. Dr. Leonard Bacon (room 76), Professor Solomon Stoddard (room 78), President Beecher, of Illinois College (room 84), President Sturtevant, of the same college (room 75), Judge

Strong, of the United States Supreme Court (room 67), Bishop Kip, of California (room 81), Professor Thacher, of New Haven, (room 90), Dr. J. P. Thompson, of Berlin (room 83). North Middle was once, so tradition has it, haunted by a ghost; but like Rip Van Winkle's canine companion, it has long since departed.

OLD CHAPEL. — The Old Chapel, standing between North Middle and North, and directly in front of the Treasury, was completed in 1824, and dedicated on the 17th of November in that year. It is built of brick, and has a front of 56 feet, and a depth of 72 feet. When new it contained on the first floor an audience-room, surrounded by a gallery, while the floor above was finished into studies and sleeping apartments for students. The attic was used for the library. A few years after the books had been removed to the new library building, this attic was occupied by the Department of Civil Engineering, which continued to have its headquarters there until the completion of Sheffield Hall in 1860. From 1824 to 1876 the structure was the college chapel, in which all the religious exercises, including daily prayers, were conducted. For years after it had been built, morning prayers were held at 6 in winter, and 5.30 in summer. In winter it was no little hardship to attend, as the room was freezing cold, the seats not the most comfortable in the world, and the thought of an immediate recitation anything but encouraging. In 1876, on the completion of Battell Chapel, the Old Chapel, as it is now called, was converted into lecture and recitation rooms. It was divided into front and rear halves by a partition built up through the centre, and the first floor front was made into a lecture-room for the President, with seats rising in tiers, and in the form of an amphitheatre. The room will seat a class of 190 or more. On the second floor front are two large recitation rooms, one used for seniors, the other for juniors. Two large recitation rooms on the first floor, and two more on the second floor, rear, are used for sophomores. The third story is still used as a dormitory. From this floor stairs and ladders lead to the belfry and

steeple, the top of the latter reaching a height of 120 feet above the
ground. Several years ago the vane which surmounted it was blown
down by a gale. Various daring feats have been performed on this
steeple by students, such as climbing to the top and fastening a freshman flag where it was supposed no sophomore would dare venture to
pull it down. Inasmuch as such a flag has about the same effect on a
sophomore that a red cloth is said to have on an enraged bull, it is
hardly necessary to remark that the flag generally came down in short
order.

Many an able preacher has spoken from the pulpit of Old Chapel,
while graduates of half a century ago recall with pleasure an address
they once heard within its walls from Daniel Webster.

NORTH COLLEGE.— North College, in the "Old Brick Row," stands
just north of Old Chapel, and partly in front of Farnam. Erected in
1821, it is the newest structure at present standing in that historic
line of buildings, with the exception of Old Chapel, built three years
later. About 106 feet long and 40 feet wide, built of brick, and four
stories high, it looks a trifle newer than either South, South Middle or
North Middle; but otherwise, and except that the roof is slated, its
appearance is about the same as that of the others. For interesting
associations, however, it is second only to South Middle, and vies with
South. Seniors at once appropriated it, on its completion, and even
now the senior class is pretty well represented there, though no one
class preponderates sufficiently to make it safe to say that it is a building usually occupied by that class. All rooms on the fourth floor are
reserved for freshmen. Years ago it was the musical centre of the College, and led in other matters. Just after it was completed, at a con-
vivial gathering of some of the occupants of the second entry, the
toast, "North Entry: the regulator, and, as it were, the pole-star of Yale
College," was drunk, showing at least what one portion of its inhabitants thought; and the members of the other entry doubtless did not
permit their end of the building to suffer by comparison. Every entry

NORTH MIDDLE.
(Page 16.)

in college, along in 1825, had one or more clubs, and jolly times they made. In that year General Lafayette visited Yale, and the seniors in North celebrated the event after his departure for Boston, whither he had gone to be present at the laying of the corner-stone of Bunker Hill monument. They raked together what money they could, bought the necessary refreshments, solid and otherwise, and had a grand feast in the attic of North, which they reached by climbing up through a trap-door. For some years the south-west corner room in North was used as a refreshment room, on the day of Junior Exhibition, in which members of the junior class entertained their lady friends. Rolling an eighteen-pound cannon-ball down the stairways of the south entry was one of the diversions indulged in while Justice Strong was an occupant of a room in North in 1827–8. The "Yale Bully Club," once one of the most famous organizations in the College, ever had its headquarters in this building. The "Bully," the appointed leader of the students, always carried a big cane or club in expeditions of the Yale men, and commanded in every battle with the townspeople, which were then of frequent occurrence, but which are now things of the past. North, too, claims the honor of originating the movement which resulted in the present Yale Literary Magazine, the oldest college publication in America.

THE SILLIMAN STATUE. — The bronze statue in the northeast angle of the campus, within a few rods of Battell Chapel and Farnam Hall, is that of one of Yale's most renowned graduates, Professor Benjamin Silliman, whose work in the cause of science gave him a world-wide fame. Much of Professor Silliman's best work was done in the old laboratory on the Yale campus. The statue, designed by Professor John F. Weir, was the gift of numerous friends of the college, to whom Professor Silliman's memory is dear, and was unveiled with proper ceremonies at Commencement, 1884.

FARNAM HALL. — Farnam Hall, the gift of Mr. Henry Farnam, of New Haven, was the first building erected within the borders of the college campus after the definite adoption of the plan of so locating all the structures in future built for the Academical Department that they should eventually form a quadrangle enclosing a hollow square. The great necessity for a new dormitory or dormitories was stated to Mr. Farnam, a friend of the College, who, in 1864, gave a large sum to be used in filling the requirement. A few years later, August 2, 1869, ground was broken on the College Street side of the campus, one hundred feet from Elm Street, on or in the vicinity of the site formerly occupied by the house built years before for the President. This house was built in 1799 and moved away in 1860. The new dormitory was completed for occupancy at the opening of the college year in 1870. Its dimensions are: 174 feet long by 37 feet wide, exclusive of projections, and four stories high, with a slated Mansard roof, from which rise two turrets used in the system of ventilation. The entrances, three in number, face the campus, a large pierced marble slab, supported by polished granite pillars, surmounting each entrance. The walls are of brick, trimmed with Hudson River bluestone and Portland freestone. There are 49 studies in the building, the great majority having two bed-rooms each, those without these appendages being nine small rooms — three leading from each section of the building — in and forming part of the projection over every entrance. Of the forty double studies, sixteen face College Street and sixteen the campus, each study having a bedroom on either side. Of the remaining eight studies there are four at each end of the building, each study facing on the campus and having its two bedrooms in the rear, facing on College Street. Every double study has a very large convenient closet, and every study in the building is supplied with steam-heat and gas, while water is conveyed by pipes to several floors. A portion of the basement, light and high, is fitted up as a residence for the janitor or sweep, while the remainder is used as a shop for the repair of gas and water pipes and heating apparatus. It was originally intended to expend about $75,000 in the construction of the building, but when finished the total expense was

very nearly $127,000. All but about $54,000 of this amount was furnished by Mr. Farnam, the College supplying the remainder. Farnam,
like Durfee, is occupied to a great extent by seniors and juniors, and
though the studies as a rule are not so expensively furnished as those
in Durfee, yet many of them are finely fitted up and very attractive.

BATTELL CHAPEL.— Battell Chapel, which occupies the northeast angle of the college campus, is one of the finest church edifices in
America, and perhaps the most costly and elegant college chapel in
the world. It forms a portion of the Yale quadrangle, and the most
satisfactory exterior view of it is obtained from a point on the north
side of Elm Street, a short distance below College Street, whence the
structure is seen in all its grand proportions. It was erected largely
through the beneficence of Mr. Joseph Battell, of New York, from
whom it takes its name, and is the third chapel erected on the college
campus for the Academical Department. It is built of rough brown
New Jersey sandstone, and is surrounded by an arcade of Ohio sandstone, which gives it a light and graceful appearance. Two massive
stone towers, capped with spires of hewn sandstone, rise from the
angles at the west end of the building, the tower facing the college
campus containing a most excellent clock: the standard by which all
exercises in the Academical Department are regulated. This clock is
connected with a peal of bells, on which it strikes the hours and
the quarters. Its single face is of hewn stone, the hands upon which
are reached from a stone balcony directly beneath it. Five large doors
furnish ample means of ingress to and egress from the chapel. On
the Elm Street side of the structure, in the transept, appears a beautiful rose window, on one side of which is a stone tablet bearing the
arms and motto of the State of Connecticut, *Qui transtulit sustinet*,
and on the other a tablet with the seal and motto of the college, *Lux
et Veritas*. The capitals of the columns supporting the arcade were
cut by hand after the walls were built, as were also the two borders of
vine-leaves in the light-colored Ohio sandstone. The interior of the

chapel will well repay a visit, and the most appropriate time would be the regular service on the Sabbath, which is held at 10.30 A.M., or perhaps better on any week-day morning at 8.10, for it is at this hour that prayers are held and an opportunity is obtained of witnessing this feature of college life and all the peculiarities attending it, while at the close of the exercises plenty of time is afforded the visitor in which to examine the building. He will observe that it consists of a nave, a north and south transept, and three galleries, one at the end of each transept, and a very large one occupying the entire west end of the chapel. The woodwork is of solid oak, elaborately carved, especially that about the pulpit and choir, where the floral sculpture is abundant and beautiful. There is more or less carved work on every pew end and arm in the chapel. Directly back of the pulpit, in the apse, stands the organ, the larger pipes in which project above the richly carved oaken screen. The banks of the organ, at which the organist sits in playing, are in the choir, immediately in front of the pulpit, the members of the choir occupying seats placed at right angles to the pulpit and facing the organist's position. Above the woodwork the brick walls appear in view and are very elaborately and richly painted and gilded. The beautiful high windows, composed of English pressed glass, are peculiarly worthy of observation. About twenty of the number are already used as memorial windows. A fitting memorial of the gentleman for whom the chapel was named, Mr. Battell, and of his sister, Mrs. Irene Larned, occupies a position on the east wall of the building, to the right of the pulpit looking from the pews. It is in the form of a metallic tablet, the inscription on which is in Latin. The auditorium contains sittings for about eleven hundred persons, the greater portion of those on the ground floor being occupied by students, and those in the galleries by members of the faculty with their families, and by visitors, who, by the way, are always welcome. The building was completed and occupied in 1876, and the total cost was about $200,000.

DURFEE HALL.—Durfee Hall, so called in honor of Mr. B. M. C. Durfee, of Fall River, Mass., to whom Yale is indebted for this structure, is generally conceded to be one of the finest, if not the finest, college dormitories in the country. It is built of New Jersey sandstone, like that used in the construction of Battell Chapel and the Art School. The trimmings are light Ohio sandstone and Hudson River bluestone. Facing on the campus, it is parallel with and a few feet from Elm Street and forms an important portion of the quadrangle, its eastern end extending to within a few feet of Battell Chapel, and its western end quite near to Alumni Hall. Its length is 181 feet, and its breadth 38 feet, except at either end, where its breadth is 40 feet. Its height is four stories, with a very sharp roof, covered with slate. The angles are crowned with small turrets, and the general appearance of the structure is grand, and pleasing to the eye. It is entered by five doorways, and contains 40 parlors or studies, each study having connected with it two bed-rooms and two large closets. All studies face on the campus and all the bed-rooms on Elm Street. The interior, finished in hard-pine, is high posted, well ventilated and comfortable, and is furnished with water, steam-heat and gas throughout. The eastern end of the basement is finished off into a dwelling for the janitor, or "sweep," as he is more familiarly called by the students. Many, and in fact nearly all the rooms occupied by students in Durfee, are excellently, and not a few of them elegantly furnished. The ornaments and decorations consist to a considerable extent, as they do in all the college dormitories, of student trophies of all sorts, from the programme of the last entertainment or the sign-board of an innocent barber, up to the prizes won in friendly contests with the members of other classes or of other colleges. Oftentimes the walls are hung with fine pictures. As a general rule the library of a room consists to a great extent of college text-books. Durfee is occupied almost wholly by seniors and juniors, the classes choosing rooms in order of rank, commencing with the seniors. It seldom or never happens that the rooms in Durfee are not all taken before the lower classes have an opportunity to choose. The rent of rooms in Durfee is higher than that in any other dormitory, occupants of the best rooms paying $220 a year. The total cost of Durfee was about $130,000.

ALUMNI HALL. — For several years previous to 1850 the College felt the need of a larger hall than any in existence on the campus at that time. Accordingly President Woolsey suggested a plan for such a building as was desired, and in 1851 ground was broken for the proposed hall in the north-west angle of the campus, within sixty or seventy feet of Elm Street, and perhaps half as far from High Street. The plan provided for a hall occupying the entire lower floor, while the second story was to be partitioned into two halls, one for the Linonian Society and the other for the Brothers Society. This plan was so far modified as to spare room in the centre of the second story for a hall for the Calliopean Society. The structure was completed in 1853, at a cost of $27,000, of which the College paid $16,000, Linonian Society $5,800, and Brothers Society $5,500. It is of red sandstone, with walls topped out in battlements, and has two towers, rising to a height of 75 feet, one on each side of the main entrance, which faces toward the east. Winding staircases within the towers lead to the society halls above, as does also a stairway in a projection in the rear, directly opposite the main entrance. For the past few years the society halls above have been used to some extent by the college musical organizations and by debating clubs; and candidates for entrance to college who cannot find seats below are examined in these rooms. These halls were at one time well fitted up by the societies. The hall below is the largest in the country, having an occupied floor above supported only by the walls. It is used principally as a place for the examination of candidates for admission and for the annual examinations of the various classes. For this purpose a hundred and fifty or more very small tables are placed about the room in such a way that no two are within several feet of each other. A little glass inkstand enclosed in a block of cork is placed on each table, as is also a lot of writing paper, and the candidates for examination are seated one at each table about the hall. Officers are stationed in elevated positions in various places around the room, and a printed copy of a list of questions is given each student, to which he writes answers as best he can. Though very few of the thousands that have entered its portals for examination have done so without fear and trembling and every sort of evil foreboding, they have generally confessed on passing out that " it was a pretty square paper, after all," the printed list of questions going by the title of " a paper." A student who has been faithful in his studies finds very little trouble in passing the examinations, while one who has shirked, and goes into the hall trusting to good fortune to carry him through, generally retires with a very high respect for the ability of the Yale faculty to unmask him, though perhaps disturbed at the amount of delving he must do before he can hope to pass. The questions on the papers are placed there to find out what a student knows, not to trip him up; and that policy is consistently carried out. No thoroughly prepared student need have any fear of an examination at Yale.

But Alumni Hall is used for other purposes than examinations; notably as a dining-hall at Commencement dinner, on which occasions it rarely happens that there are not several of the leading men of the country present, when " a feast of reason and a flow of soul" is sure to follow the repast of meat and drink.

During the spring of 1881, through the munificence of Mrs. Henry Farnam, of New Haven, the interior of Alumni Hall was elegantly improved. A handsome new floor was laid, wainscotting was placed on the walls to a height of eight feet, the ceiling was panelled, a small gallery was built over the main entrance, and a platform for Commencement and other speakers placed directly opposite. The whole is painted in the dark shades so much in vogue, and new stained-glass windows complete the improvements which have added so greatly to the appearance of the hall.

STEAM-HEATING WORKS.—Rising a few feet above the surface of the ground, in the extreme northwestern angle of the campus, near Alumni Hall, is a very modest-looking hatchway which leads down to the subterranean boiler rooms, where the steam is generated which heats not only Durfee, Farnam, North, North Middle, Battell Chapel, Old Chapel, Treasury, Library and the Old Laboratory, but the great Peabody Museum as well, and the system is undergoing constant extension. The steam passes through iron pipes, properly encased in a non-conductor of heat and buried in the ground. To those interested in improved mechanical appliances, and in proposed methods of heating large numbers of buildings from a single source, the boiler vault is worth a visit.

SANITARY ARRANGEMENTS.—Also concerning mechanical appliances and other arrangements for the health and comfort of the students, it may be stated that everything on the campus or connected with the Academical Department in the line of sewers and plumbing is a triumph of sanitary engineering. The present system was put in in the summer of 1881, at an expense of $10,000, according to the plans of Colonel George E. Waring, and under the direction of men approved by him.

THE TREASURY.—The Treasury is immediately west of the Old Chapel, and was built in 1832, for a gallery wherein to place the historical paintings of Colonel Trumbull, which that gentleman had given to the College with the proviso that they should be exhibited for a small fee, the proceeds to be used in aiding indigent students. The material in the building is brick covered with brownish stucco, and the length is 65 feet and width 35 feet, with a height of two stories. The second story served its purpose as an art gallery until 1868, when the paintings were removed to the beautiful new Art Building. Windows were cut through, after the removal of the pictures, and the southern half of the second floor is now used for the treasury, and contains a

ATHENÆUM.
(Page 13.)

OLD CHAPEL.
(Page 17.)

LYCEUM.
(Page 15.)

BERZELIUS HALL.
(Page 41.)

strong vault, appropriate to the purpose, while the northern half contains the President's office and room in which the academical faculty holds its weekly meetings. For years the room beneath the president's office was used as a store-room for mineralogical specimens, which have since been removed to Peabody Museum. The room for a time served as a zoological laboratory. The room under the eastern portion of the treasurer's office is occupied by students, and that under the western portion is the headquarters of the superintendent of grounds and buildings. The Treasury appropriately enough has a massive, tomb-like appearance, for beneath it were buried the remains of Colonel and Mrs. Trumbull, at the request of the former of whom they were there interred.

THE LIBRARY. — The Library, occupying a position on the High Street side of the campus, midway between Chapel and Elm streets, was completed in 1846, work having been begun upon it in 1843. For years previous to that time the necessity for a library building had been acknowledged, and this feeling at length resulted in a movement toward obtaining the necessary funds. Eighteen thousand dollars was raised by subscription, of which Professor Salisbury gave $6,000, President Woolsey $3,000, Rev. Cortlandt Van Rensselaer $600, and President Day, Professor Goodrich, Henry D. A. Ward, and Hon. Thomas S. Williams $500 each. The total cost of the building was $34,000. It is of brown sandstone, taken from the Portland quarries, and has a frontage of 151 feet, from the extreme northern to the extreme southern wall. It is composed of a main hall in the centre, which is connected by wings with smaller halls on each side. From the angles of the main hall towers rise to a height of 91 feet. The interior dimensions of this hall are 41 × 83 feet; of the connecting wings, 26 × 40 feet; and of the side halls, 20 × 56 feet. The southern hall and wing are used for storage of unbound pamphlets, duplicates, etc., the main hall for the works belonging to the library proper; the northern wing for an entrance to the main hall and for an office for the librarian and the secretary, and the northern hall for the library of the Linonian and the Brothers societies, literary organizations that flourished in the College for nearly a century, each of which owned, in 1870, a library of 13,000 volumes. In 1871 both these libraries were placed under the charge of the college library committee, were consolidated, and now form a department of the college library, though kept entirely distinct from the main library, the card system being used in that, while the catalogue system serves in the society library, which is more generally used by the students of all departments of the University than the main library or any of the professional department libraries, containing as it does all the best current literature and works usually called for in a public library. The library, with its various branches, has grown with wonderful rapidity, and now contains, inclusive of unbound works, about 200,000 volumes, the main library containing, exclusive of unbound works, about 108,000 volumes, Linonian and Brothers library about 24,000 volumes, and the libraries of the professional schools about 23,000 volumes. The visitor to the main library will find, in addition to the books, many curious and valuable manuscripts, inscriptions, etc., not accessible elsewhere; also Franklin's clock, Rector Pierson's chair, and many other articles of interest. At various points in the main hall are busts of benefactors of the College, while marble tablets on the end toward the campus are inscribed with the names of the principal donors to the library. To their munificence largely is due the remarkable increase of the main library from 21,000 volumes in 1850 to 35,000 volumes in 1860; 55,000 volumes in 1870, 80,000 volumes in 1876, and 108,000 volumes in 1881. It is open daily in term time from 9.30 A.M. to 1 P.M., and from 2.30 to 5 P.M. (or during winter months, to 4.30 P.M.) Linonian and Brothers is open daily from 1.30 to 2.30 P.M.; on Wednesdays and Saturdays from 10 A.M. to 12 M., and from 1.30 to 4 P.M. Visitors are welcome. When leaving the building it will be worth while to observe the beautiful class ivies growing on the extreme northern and other walls of the structure, planted there

by the classes at graduation. The ivies are distinguished by the class
numeral cut in the stone wall, in the immediate vicinity of the vine, a
foot or two above the ground. Graduates on returning to the scenes
of their college life seldom fail to visit the spot where, in the fast-
gathering shades of evening, the class assembled for the last time with
unbroken ranks and carefully deposited in the fostering soil the final
memento of happy days at Yale.

THE READING-ROOM.—The Philosophical Building, or Reading-Room as it is more familiarly called, occupies a position about a
hundred feet in the rear of the Lyceum. It is two stories high, with
light basement, is built of brick covered with stucco and is 86 feet long
by 45 feet broad. Erected in 1819 for a dining-hall or commons, it
continued to serve that purpose until the abolition of a college commons in 1843. While it was used for commons the cooking department
was in the basement and the dining-room occupied the first floor; the
second floor served as a mineralogical cabinet. After 1843, for many
years the first floor was taken up by the "philosophical chamber,"
which still occupies the entire southern half of this story, and by two
sophomore recitation rooms. At present the northeastern portion of
this floor is used as a junior recitation room and the northwestern
portion as a repository for physical apparatus. When the northern
wing of Peabody Museum was completed, the mineralogical cabinet
was transferred to that building and the entire second floor of the
Philosophical Building is now occupied by the Reading-Room. It is
by long odds the best equipped college reading-room in America,
containing all the most prominent dailies, weeklies and periodicals,
American and foreign. Duplicate copies of metropolitan papers
are always on the files. Numerous windows on each of the four sides
of the building afford an abundance of light, the room is high-posted
and airy, the walls are adorned with steel engravings, and everything
combines to make it one of the most agreeable institutions of the
College. Visitors will derive much pleasure from an inspection of it.

The room is open on week-days from 9.30 A.M. to 8 P.M., and on Sundays from 1 P.M. to 8 P.M.

LAWRENCE HALL. — For some years the college has greatly needed additional dormitories, and at the annual meeting of the alumni, in 1883, it was announced that the corporation had appointed a committee to present a plan for a building of that class. But there were no funds. A few months after that time, however, Mr. and Mrs. William C. Lawrence of New York, made a spontaneous gift of $50,000 for that purpose. The building is designed by them as a memorial of their son, Thomas Garner Lawrence, a member of the class of 1884, whose lamented death occurred in New Haven soon after the beginning of his senior year. The plan contemplates rooms for about eighty of the two hundred and fifty students who have hitherto been unable to find lodgings in the college.

LABORATORY. — The Chemical and Physical Laboratory, standing back of the Athenæum, is the most ancient building of any on the campus, with the exception of South Middle and the Athenæum. It is of brick, painted dingy white, and is 90 feet long, 30 feet wide, and a story and a half high. It was originally intended for a dining-hall and kitchen for the students, and was used for that purpose until 1819, when the dining-room was removed to the new building erected for the purpose, and now known as the Reading-Room or Philosophical Building, standing between the Laboratory and the Treasury. Since 1819 the Laboratory has been used for what its present name indicates. It contains a large lecture-room, with seats in tiers, and will comfortably accommodate one hundred or more persons. The north-western portion of the edifice is an addition to the original building, and contains an office, store-room, chemical and physical apparatus, etc. For a time the northeastern portion was occupied as a residence by the janitor of one of the buildings. It is restricted to the use of the Chemical Department since the completion of the beautiful new laboratory promised on behalf of two friends of the College at the annual alumni dinner in 1881. Still it will long be remembered as the spot where the world-renowned Professor Silliman performed his works for the benefit of science, and made a number of his most celebrated experiments. Though the building is in its external appearance the most unattractive of any on the grounds, it nevertheless " in its time has been," as the Yale Book says, "one of the most important centres of chemical science in America, and the scene of a great educational work. A long list could be made of eminent instructors and investigators in science, who received their first impulses toward a scientific career, and in many instances a large share of their professional training, within its walls."

The handsome great building of sandstone, just west of the Laboratory, is the Yale School of the Fine Arts, a description of which appears on page 52.

STATUE OF RECTOR PIERSON. — The bronze statue a short distance south of the Old Laboratory is that of Abraham Pierson, the first President of Yale College, and was erected with appropriate ceremonies at Commencement in 1874. It was designed by Launt Thompson, and presented to the college by Mr. Charles Morgan of New York. On the front of the granite pedestal upon which the statue rests are inscribed, in Latin, the name and date of office of Rector Pierson, while on the reverse, also in Latin, appear the name and residence of the donor of the statue, with the date of erection of the same. As the artist had no likeness of Rector Pierson from which to work, the features in the statue are almost wholly ideal, though some assistance was secured from portraits of members of the Pierson family. The statue represents the Rector clad in the dress of two hundred years ago, the robe of office falling in graceful folds from the shoulders to the feet. The left hand rests easily at the side, while the right clasps a book to the breast. A firm, determined, yet kindly look, is borne upon the features, which are directed straight ahead, as though

forecasting the mighty **power of the** future University for **all that is**
loftiest and best in the education of mankind.

SKULL AND BONES HALL.—Skull and Bones Hall on High
Street, directly opposite the northwestern wing of the Art School, is a
plain, massive-looking structure of brown sandstone, standing in the
centre of a lot held in trust for the society occupying the building.
To the gaze of the observer the edifice seems to be entirely cut off from
light as far as the interior is concerned, inasmuch as there are no
windows to be seen, and the doors, made of iron, are ponderous and
close-fitting, affording no opportunity for light to penetrate in that
direction, while a luxuriant Virginia creeper covers with its dense foliage the entire front of the hall, scarcely excepting the massive doors.
The hall was erected in 1856, and has a front of 33 feet and a depth
of 44 feet, and is in the neighborhood of 30 feet in height. Ventilators
and chimneys rise from the edge of the roof, which is covered with
plates of iron half an inch in thickness. Two blind windows in the
rear of the building are very firmly barred, as are also the scuttle-
holes just above the foundation, everything about the structure presenting the appearance of strength and solidity. It is occupied by the
famous senior society known as Skull and Bones. This association
was organized in 1832 by fifteen members of the class of 1833, one of
whom is now Ex-Attorney General Taft. Fifteen members are elected
from every senior class, the elections being given out a short time
previous to Commencement in junior year. Early evening is the time
chosen for notifying of their election the men that have been chosen,
and several hundred students, and ladies with their escorts, always
gather on the campus, between North College and Durfee, to witness
the ceremony. The members proceed from the hall one at a time,
search among the students for the ones elected, and on finding them
touch them on the shoulder and ask them to go to their rooms, whither
they are followed and given a formal offer of election, which is practically always accepted. Those of the men elected who are popular

among their associates are heartily cheered and congratulated by their classmates and friends, as an election to the society is looked upon as one of the greatest student honors in the entire course. As a rule, of the fifteen members chosen, two are editors of the Yale Literary Magazine, one or two are chosen from each of the three great athletic interests—base-ball, foot-ball and boating—one from the staff of each of the Yale newspapers, one or more for high scholarship, and so on, the intention being, apparently, to secure representative men from all the leading student interests in the class. The society has on its roll the names of some of the ablest men in the country, including Hon. Alphonzo Taft, and Hon. William M. Evarts.

THE SLOANE PHYSICAL LABORATORY. — The Sloane Physical Laboratory on the south side of Library Street, directly opposite the Gymnasium, was completed early in 1884, and is a beautiful large brick building of the style of the German renaissance. A large, tall octagonal tower, modeled after that of the Town Hall at Altenburg, and provided with an iron balcony near the top, rises from the angle formed by the two wings. The entrance is through the lower part of this tower and leads to what is undoubtedly the most elegant and thoroughly appointed physical laboratory in the United States. The wing facing on Library Street is taken up largely with recitation and lecture rooms. To the left of the entrance, in the south wing, is a beautiful lecture room, high, light and commodious, and capable of accommodating a large class. The lecturer's table is built with especial reference to practical illustrations of the subject taught, and everything is at hand for convenience in making experiments. The portion of the building west of this lecture hall, is filled with apparatus rooms and laboratories provided with ample facilities for practical work, as well as for original investigation in the department of science to which the building is devoted. Yale is indebted for this laboratory to the munificence of Mr. Henry T. Sloane of the class of 1866 and Mr. Thomas C. Sloane of the class of 1868. The building was finished and occupied early in 1884, and is in complete accord with the suggestions and ideas of Professor A. W. Wright. Previous to the erection of the Sloane Laboratory the department had been obliged to content itself with what is now known among the students as the "Old Lab," and none can better appreciate the Sloane Laboratory than Professor Wright and the thousands of graduates who, in years gone by, were familiar with its ancient predecessor.

THE GYMNASIUM. — Standing on Library Street, a little west of High, is a plain brick structure, 100 feet long by 50 wide, and two stories high, with well-lighted basement extending under the entire structure. This building is the Gymnasium. The principal room, on the first floor, contains horizontal bars, ladders, trapezes, spring-boards, lifting-machines, weights, dumb-bells, etc., etc., while the basement contains the bath-rooms, heating apparatus, bowling-alleys, hydraulic rowing-machines (for the University crew), and a wire-enclosed room for base-ball practice.

DELTA KAPPA EPSILON HALL. — The Delta Kappa Epsilon Hall occupies a lot of land on the eastern side of York Street, a few steps south of Elm Street. It has a frontage of 24 feet 6 inches, and a depth of 45 feet, with a height of something over 30 feet. The building is of brick, and was erected for solidity and strength rather than beauty, apparently, as there are few attempts at ornamentation. A slab of brown sandstone above the entrance has carved into its surface the letters *Δ. K. E.*, and the chapter letter *Φ*, is located just above the door. The hall was erected in 1861, and is valued probably at from $8,000 to $10,000. The society to which it belongs is controlled by juniors exclusively. Meetings are held on Tuesday evenings, when, so Dame Rumor has it,— for the proceedings in all the society halls at Yale are secret — literary exercises occur and a lunch is partaken of. Once in every term, quite an elaborate programme is prepared, including one or two short plays, speeches, etc., full of jokes concerning college

FARNAM HALL
(Page 19.)

DURFEE HALL.
(Page 21.)

affairs of every sort. This is no secret, as copies of the printed pro-
grammes are exhibited at the members' rooms, without any attempt at
concealment. An unusually good supper accompanies such occasions.
As to the interior construction of the society halls at Yale, there is of
course nothing known about it except what parties who saw the various buildings while in course of construction say, which is, that these
edifices are divided into an upper and a lower hall — the upper hall
being used, it is supposed, as a theatre, and the lower one as a place
for holding meetings. *Δ. K. E.* like its rival, Psi Upsilon, chooses
about forty members from each junior class and gives out its elections
in precisely the way stated in the article describing *Ψ. Y.* hall. The
Yale chapter of *Δ. K. E.*, which is the parent chapter of the fraternity,
was organized in 1844. Charlton T. Lewis, Gen. J. W. Swayne, Brig.-
Gen. J. T. Croxton and Professor Cyrus Northrop are among the distinguished gentlemen whose names are enrolled on the list of members
of the Yale chapter.

Going a few steps north of *Δ. K. E.* Hall and turning down Elm
Street, the very tall brick structure seen on the right hand side of the
street, one block below York Street, is Peabody Museum, a description
of which is given on page 58.

PSI **UPSILON** HALL. — The Psi Upsilon Hall, on the western
side of High Street; a short distance from Elm, was completed in
1870. It has a front of 26 feet, a depth of 66 feet, and is something
over thirty feet high. The material of the walls is brick, ornamented
with freestone trimmings, the latter including the projection at the
entrance and the sill and cap of the window in the centre of the second story front. A Mansard roof, under which is a handsome cornice,
and above which is an ornamental railing of iron, adorns the front of
the edifice and gives it a light, tasteful appearance. Three bands of
dark-colored tiles — one just above the foundation, the next at the
beginning of the second story, and the third directly beneath the
cornice — add to the beauty of the pressed-brick front. The freestone

slab above the doors, which are of oak, bears in relief the Greek letters *Ψ. Y.*, while the keystone above the window over the entrance bears in relief the Greek letter *B*, indicating that the hall is owned by the Beta chapter of the fraternity. Psi Upsilon at Yale is a junior society, and about forty members of every junior class are elected to membership in the organization. Meetings are held on the Tuesday evenings in term time, and the elections are given out two or three weeks before Commencement. On that occasion the members form in line, two deep, and, preceded by a calcium light borne on a wooden frame by four members of the society, march around to and visit various rooms, in each of which a certain number of men pledged to join the society are awaiting their coming. The procession files through the room, each member shaking hands with each candidate, and receiving, on marching out again, two or three fine cigars, presented by the newly-elected members. The other junior society, *Δ. K. E.*, is always out on the same mission, under precisely similar circumstances. Accident or design, or both, always cause the two processions to pass each other several times during the evening, and each, singing its own society song, attempts to the best of its ability to drown the voices of the other. It is always done with the utmost good nature, and both sides enjoy it heartily, as do also the numerous spectators. The hall of Psi Upsilon was planned by Mr. David R. Brown, and cost about $15,000. Among the prominent gentlemen who have been members of the *Ψ. Y.* at Yale are Rev. H. M. Dexter, Henry Stevens, F. S. A., ex-Senator O. S. Ferry, President White of Cornell, Chauncey M. Depew, and Eugene Schuyler. The Yale chapter was organized in 1838.

Continuing his walk along High Street to Wall Street, and passing down the latter thoroughfare to College Street, the visitor will observe on the northwest corner the structure known as Scroll and Key Hall. The square, brick school-house on the northwest corner of High and Wall streets, which the visitor passes *en route* to Scroll and Key Hall, is the Hopkins Grammar School, described elsewhere in the portion of the book concerning New Haven.

SCROLL AND KEY HALL. — Scroll and Key Hall, on the north-west corner of College and Wall streets, is among the handsomest, most tasteful and costly college-society buildings in America. Standing in the centre of a lot 48 by 92 feet, the edifice has a front of 36 feet, and a depth of 55 feet, with a height of about 35 feet. It is built of yellow Cleveland stone, ornamented with dark blue marble. Four marble-capped pillars of Aberdeen granite sustain three arches on the front of, and above the entrance to, the structure. Within each arch is a window-shaped opening, through apertures in which ventilation is secured. Five similar, though not projecting arches, each enclosing the window-like opening just described, adorn either side of the hall, these greater arches surmounting five smaller ones located just above the surface of the ground. The entrance, approached from either side by a flight of Cleveland-stone steps, is protected by a pair of massive iron doors, made to look lighter than they really are by iron lattice-work. Stone pillars surmount the walls, and slabs of stone, each perforated with star-shaped orifices, fill the spaces between these pillars, thus forming a coping which entirely conceals the chimneys, ventilators, etc., from view. A handsome iron fence, having stone posts at the angles and at either side of the gate, separates the lot, on which the hall stands, from the highway. The entire property must be worth at least $50,000. The architect was Mr. Richard M. Hunt, of New York. Scroll and Key, like Skull and Bones, is a senior society, and as far as can be seen by the public, is very similar to it, each choosing fifteen members from every senior class, each giving out its elections in the same way, each holding its regular meetings on the same evening — Thursday — and each striving to secure the leading men in the class. Scroll and Key was organized in 1841 by members of the class of 1842, among whom was John A. Porter. Its list contains the names of quite a number of gentlemen well known to the public, including Charlton T. Lewis and Mason Young, Esq.

The Scientific Department.

Sketch of its History. — At the northern extremity of College Street, just one block from Scroll and Key Hall, and a few minutes' walk from the grounds of the Academical Department, is located the world-renowned Sheffield Scientific School. The Scientific Department of Yale College had its origin in 1846, when the college corporation voted to establish a professorship in agricultural chemistry and one in analytical chemistry. In 1847 the actual work of the department began. The residence on the campus formerly occupied by the President, and standing on the site now occupied by Farnam Hall, was fitted up for a laboratory, and the professors began their duties, with few students and less money. Eight was the exact number of students. Messrs. John Pitkin Norton and Benjamin Silliman, Jr., were the first professors. In 1849 Professor Silliman accepted a position elsewhere, and for a time Professor Norton carried on the work alone. His intense zeal for science and for the department founded upon it brought him to a premature death, in 1852. He had demonstrated the value of such a school, however, and from that moment the department became a recognized advantage to the University. For several years the struggle for absolutely necessary funds was a severe one, and it was not until 1859 that relief came, when Mr. Joseph E. Sheffield, who had become acquainted with the workings of the department through his son-in-law, Professor John A. Porter, purchased the building at the northern end of College Street, formerly used by the Medical Department, and presented it to the Scientific Department, first having thoroughly repaired, refitted and enlarged the structure, which is now known as Sheffield Hall. The departments of Analytical and Agricultural Chemistry and of Civil Engineering, which latter, by the way, had been established in 1852, moved into the new quarters in 1860; and at the Commencement of 1861 the corporation gave to these combined departments the name of the Sheffield Scientific School, out of gratitude to the generosity of its benefactor who, not content with presenting a building, had given $50,000 for the endowment of professorships. In 1861 the system of entrance examinations went into effect, and in the same year the time for completing the course was lengthened from two years to three. In 1863 this department was made to embrace the Connecticut Agricultural College, which gave it the income of $135,000, and aided it exceedingly. Professorships have been added to this department one by one, and its faculty now numbers no less than twenty-five professors and instructors, while its list of students has increased from about twenty in 1861, and seventy-five in 1871, to over two hundred in 1881. These figures indicate more forcibly and plainly than words can the great success of the Sheffield Scientific School. It has advantages possessed by no similar institution in the world, its wide-spread influence and renown and the great number applying for instruction at the suggestion of the most eminent practical men, being sufficient guarantee of the truth of this statement. Its graduates are in great demand — in fact, the degree or certificate issued is recognized among scientific men everywhere as a sufficient guarantee of the ability of the graduate to perform any duty for which the certificate states that he is fitted. Never before has so proud a reputation been won in so short a time as that on all sides conceded to the Sheffield Scientific School of Yale University.

The entrance examination in the Scientific Department comprises the following subjects :—

English, including grammar, spelling and composition.

History of the United States.

Geography.

Latin — **Six books of** Cæsar's Commentaries.

Arithmetic, including the metric system.

Algebra — Up to the general theory of equations.

Geometry — Plane, solid and **spherical** — **equivalent to** the nine books in Chauvenet's Treatise.

Trigonometry — so much as is contained in Richards's or Wheeler's Plane Trigonometry.

SHEFFIELD HALL.— Sheffield Hall, the first building **owned by** the Scientific Department, stands on the corner of Grove and **Prospect** streets, and was formerly occupied by the Medical Department. Previous to **that time it was a hotel.** It originally consisted of a three-story, stone building, stuccoed, and was 53 feet square. After Mr. Sheffield purchased the structure for the Scientific School, in 1859, he **caused a wing to be added to each** side of it, "that on the west for chemical laboratories, and that on the east for engineering **and metallurgy.**" To accommodate the increased number **of students, Mr. Shef-**field again, in 1865, "enlarged it, **and made changes. An addition** three stories high, filling the rear court and extending beyond **it, was built,** containing an additional chemical laboratory, lecture-room **and a** library **room.** A projecting observatory-tower was put on in front, about ninety feet high, containing a public clock, and surmounted by a revolving turret containing a large telescope equatorially mounted. Another and lower projecting tower, with massive interior pier, was added at the northwest corner, containing a large meridian circle. As it now stands, the building has an extreme length of 117 feet and a depth of 112 feet, the whole representing a series of adaptations and **growths.**" It is chiefly used for chemical laboratories, though it con-**tains** the library, map-room, a number of lecture-rooms, **etc.** The first **floor of the eastern wing is taken up by the** Connecticut Agriculture **Experiment Station, where is located the** necessary apparatus for **making the various tests and** experiments connected with the service **of scientific farming.**

NORTH SHEFFIELD HALL.—North Sheffield Hall occupies the lot on Prospect Street, a short distance north of Sheffield Hall. Like Sheffield Hall, it was given to the department by its great benefactor, Mr. Joseph E. Sheffield, and was planned by members of the faculty selected by Mr. Sheffield for the purpose. It is built of brick, with brown-stone foundation and blue-stone trimmings. The walls are inlaid with white and blue bricks disposed in tasteful patterns, bands of these patterns running around the entire building, the first band just above the sill of the windows in the first story and the next near the top of the second-story windows, while several bands encircle the third story. The roof of the building is flat. A handsome portico over the front entrance is supported by stone pillars surmounted by beautifully-wrought capitals. The exterior dimensions of the building are 84 × 76 feet, and it is practically five stories high, the basement being entirely above ground and finely lighted. The interior is excellently finished and contains recitation rooms, lecture rooms, and work-shop, with all apparatus belonging and pertaining to drawing, civil and dynamical engineering, physics, and botany. North Sheffield Hall is one of the most thoroughly built, convenient and attractive buildings in the University, and has no superior anywhere for the purpose for which it was built. Its cost was about $100,000. The architect was Mr. J. C. Cady, of New York.

BERZELIUS HALL.—Berzelius Hall, the only structure thus far built exclusively for a secret society connected with the Scientific Department, is on the westerly side of Prospect Street, a short distance north of the New Haven and Northampton Railroad. It is very peculiar in appearance, having a front composed of bricks of light shades, disposed in a massive arch over the entrance, a series of small supporting arches at the point of union of the first and second stories, three window-shaped arches in the second story, and a heavy cornice at the top. The massive doors of oak, with grotesque fastenings, accord excellently with the appearance of strength stamped

on every portion of the building. The side and rear walls are solidly
built of red brick, and afford little or no encouragement to any one who
might feel disposed to gain unlawful admittance to the interior of the
edifice. The society to which the hall belongs is as old as the Scientific Department itself, having been organized in 1848. Its active
members are men chosen from the senior and junior classes, and vary
in number from year to year; but the average membership is about
twelve. The hall was completed in 1876 at a cost of about $9,000.

THIRD SENIOR SOCIETY HALL. — In this immediate vicinity,
on the corner of Prospect and Trumbull streets, stands the Third
Senior Society Hall of the Academical Department. In the early
summer of 1883 a number of members from each of the classes '83
and '84, deeming the establishment of a new senior society to be
desirable on account of the largely increased numbers in the classes
and for other reasons, held a meeting for consultation. After much
careful thought, and with the advice of graduates and friends of the
college, the project was deemed an excellent one. Vigorous measures
were at once taken, the lot on which the building stands was purchased,
and before cold weather had arrived the foundation was laid and ready
for the superstructure. In the summer of 1884 the building was completed, ready for occupancy. It is two and a half stories high, built
of brown sandstone, and is arranged with every facility for comfort and
convenience. The new hall differs radically from all other society
buildings in the college in that it is abundantly lighted from the exterior
by numerous windows. The society is composed of fifteen members
from each senior class.

THE THEOLOGICAL DEPARTMENT.

SKETCH OF ITS HISTORY. — This department of the University virtually dates its organization from the very formation of Yale, owing to the facts (1) that the College was originated by clergymen, and (2) for over a century theology was one of the chief studies of the regular college course. The formal organization of a separate department in theology, however, occurred in 1822. In 1835 a building closely resembling North College was erected just north of the latter structure for the theological students, and was used for that purpose until 1870, when it was demolished. In 1867 the degree of Bachelor of Divinity was first given to those who had completed the full course of three years. At that time there were in the department but few if any over a dozen students, but the growth in the past ten years has been exceedingly rapid, and the department has had an average for the past three years of about one hundred students. Including special lecturers the board of instruction in this department numbers fifteen. There are seven full professorships. The special lecturers are chosen from the ablest pulpit orators and specialists in the world, and the list has included such men as Rev. Robert W. Dale, D.D.; Rev. John Hall, D.D.; Rev. Phillips Brooks, D.D.; Rev. Howard Crosby, D.D., LL.D.; Prof. Asa Gray, LL.D.; Rev. Joseph T. Duryea, D.D.; and the Rev. William M. Taylor, D.D.

In 1879 the Theological Department of Yale College instituted a graduate class, "designed to be composed of students who have finished a full theological course of three years in this Divinity School or some similar institution, and who desire to pursue an advanced course of study for one or more years. It was the first Divinity School in the country to make systematic provision for such an advanced course, beyond the limits of the regular curriculum."

The conditions of admission to this department are membership in some evangelical church, or other satisfactory evidence of Christian character, and a liberal education at some college, or, in exceptional cases, an equivalent preparation for theological studies. Students of every Christian denomination, in case they are possessed of these qualifications, are admitted.

EAST DIVINITY HALL.—This very large and beautiful dormitory, standing on the corner of Elm and College streets, was completed in 1870, at a cost of about $180,000. It is built of brick, trimmed with Nova Scotia stone, and has a height of five stories at the wings, and four along the middle portion. The length of the building is 164 feet, and width 43 feet. Mr. Richard M. Hunt, of New York, was the architect. The first floor is taken up by lecture and reading rooms, corridors, janitor's residence, etc., while the floors above contain about fifty studies, with each of which a bed-room connects. As a general rule each student has a study to himself. Every room in the building is very high-posted, light and pleasant, contains a fire-place, and is capable of being made as comfortable as anyone could desire. The lecture-rooms, etc., on the first floor are nearly always open for inspection. As the visitor is passing out along the corridor, toward Elm Street, he will find an entrance to the beautiful little edifice known as:—

MARQUAND CHAPEL.—It faces on Elm Street and is just west of East Divinity Hall, with which it connects by a wing. It is of brick, trimmed with Nova Scotia stone, and has a very high, steep roof, ornamented with iron trimmings. The interior is finished in Southern pine, beautifully carved and decorated, and contains sittings for two or three hundred persons. The cost of this chapel was about $25,000, all of

BATTELL CHAPEL.
(Page 21.)

ALUMNI HALL.

which was the gift of Frederick Marquand, from whom it takes its name.

WEST DIVINITY HALL.— West Divinity Hall, parallel with, and about a hundred feet west of East Divinity, on Elm Street, very closely resembles the latter hall in general appearance, both outside and inside, though studies take the place, in this building, of the lecture-rooms, etc., on the first floor of East Divinity. West Divinity contains in all nearly seventy rooms, quite a number of which accommodate two students each. West Divinity was built in 1873-4, to accommodate the increasing number of theological students. The rooms not taken by them are occupied by members of the Academical and Scientific Departments. Perhaps half the students in this building are students in these last-mentioned departments. All students in East Divinity are members of the Theological Department. West Divinity was completed in 1874 at a cost of about $160,000, of which Mr. Frederick Marquand gave one-half.

TROWBRIDGE LIBRARY BUILDING.— The Library, a substantial brick structure on Elm Street, just east of and connected with West Divinity Hall, is the newest of the buildings belonging to the Theological Department, having been completed in the fall of 1881. It is of brick, trimmed with Nova Scotia stone, and has a front of 32 feet, and a depth of 50 feet, while the extreme height of the ceiling is 40 feet. The windows are of hammered glass of cathedral pattern and of neutral tints bordered with glass of more positive colors. The wood-work is mostly of oak, finished in oil, though the ceiling, which is arched, is worked in white pine and matched panels, and is finished in shellac and varnish. A gallery extending around three sides of the room is reached by a stairway leading from an alcove at the west side of the building. The book-cases are of oak, beautifully carved, and finished in oil, and contain the reference library of the Theological Department and the famous Lowell Mason library of church music, presented to the Yale Theological Department by Mr. Mason's family. By an admirable arrangement of windows all the cases are excellently lighted. A handsome carpet and costly furniture complete the equipage of the edifice, which is the most elegant theological library building in the United States. It was the gift of Mr. Frederick Marquand, and cost $10,500. The architect was Mr. R. M. Hunt, of New York. The Trowbridge Library completes the Elm Street front of the buildings of the Theological Department.

At this point it may be well to call the attention of the visitor to : —

CENTRE CHURCH. — Centre Church, on the city green, midway between Chapel and Elm streets, and facing on Temple Street, is and has been so intimately associated with the University that a brief description of it will not be out of place in a work concerning Yale, for continuously since 1717, with the exception of two years when the present edifice was in course of construction, the exercises at Commencement have been observed in the house of worship owned by the society to which belongs the Centre Church. The building is of brick, with shingled roof, and has a tall, handsome wooden spire surmounted by a gilded vane. Doric pillars support the porch surrounding the brick tower from which the spire rises. Above and on each side of the arched window over the principal entrance to the church are marble tablets, containing the following inscriptions in large letters :—

QUINNIPIAC CHOSEN FOR SETTLEMENT, A.D. 1637.

———

THE WILDERNESS AND THE SOLITARY PLACE SHALL BE MADE GLAD FOR THEM.

———

O GOD OF HOSTS LOOK DOWN FROM HEAVEN AND BEHOLD AND VISIT THIS VINE.

A.D. 1638 A COMPANY OF ENGLISH CHRISTIANS LED BY JOHN DAVEN-
PORT AND THEOPHILUS EATON WERE THE FOUNDERS OF THIS CITY.
HERE THEIR EARLIEST HOUSE OF WORSHIP WAS BUILT A.D. 1639.

THE FIRST CHURCH BEGINNING WITH WORSHIP IN THE OPEN AIR APRIL
15 [O. S.], 1638, WAS THE BEGINNING OF NEW HAVEN, AND WAS
ORGANIZED AUG. 22 [O. S.], 1639. THIS HOUSE WAS DEDICATED
TO THE WORSHIP OF GOD IN CHRIST DEC. 27, 1814.

The site of Centre Church was once a burying-ground. When the
structure was built the graves were undisturbed, and are there to this
day. Among the remains interred within the space enclosed by its
walls are those of some of the first settlers of New Haven colony.
Recently the basement has been arranged so that access to the crypt
is convenient, and the church is open for that purpose every Saturday.
The vestibule of the edifice contains marble tablets on which are
inscribed the names of those buried beneath the building. Immediately in the rear of the church, surrounded by an iron fence, a sub-
stantial-looking marble monument marks the spot where were buried
the remains of the British regicide John Dixwell, who fled to the colony
for protection after 1661.

From this point it is but a moment's walk down to Church Street,
just north of Court Street, where are situated the apartments occupied
by :—

THE LAW DEPARTMENT.

SKETCH OF ITS HISTORY. — The Yale Law School, on Church Street, was organized in 1822, and has had in all not far from 2,000 students. The degree of Bachelor of Law was first conferred in 1843. From the date of its organization the school has ever held a high rank; and never more so than at present. Its undergraduate course is thorough and complete, occupying two full college years, while its graduate course is entirely unique in America, and offers instruction sought by graduates of all the leading law schools of the country. This course "has created at Yale a school of political science, the first one instituted in the United States, and the only one yet in full operation. Regular instruction is given in American and English Constitutional history, the formation and regulation of municipal corporations, international law, political economy, parliamentary law, canon law, general and comparative jurisprudence, Roman and French law, sociology, and conflict of laws, besides other topics of more immediate importance to the practising lawyer." The library of the school contains all the English and American (including the Canadian) reports, a good collection of statutes and digests, and a large number of text-books and books of reference, including many works upon Roman and French law. The whole number of volumes is upwards of 8,000, constituting by far the best library, with one exception, of any American law school. The faculty of the law school consists of five professors and three lecturers.

Applicants for admission to the junior class must be at least eighteen years of age, and must produce certificates of good moral character.

No student who has not taken a degree from some collegiate institution will be admitted as a candidate for a degree until he has passed a satisfactory examination on the outlines of the history of England and of the United States, and the text of the Constitution of the United States. This will be conducted in writing, and the style of composition and orthography in the answers, as written, must be such as to evince a competent knowledge of English grammar.

THE LAW-SCHOOL BUILDING. — The Yale Law School is located on Church Street, just north of Court Street, in a handsome brownstone edifice which it occupies in connection with the courts of New Haven County. This building was completed for occupancy by the school in 1873. Previous to that time the headquarters of this department of the University were in the Leffingwell Building, on the corner of Church and Court streets. All 'things considered, no law school in America is so admirably located for its special purposes as that at Yale. Occupying "an entire story of the building and having upon the same floor a lecture-room accommodating two hundred students, a large library hall, a moot court-room, an instructors' room, and other apartments containing every convenience for law clubs and debating societies," it is literally in the midst of courts, located in the same edifice. Two terms of the Supreme Court of Errors of Connecticut are annually held there, and the Superior Court and Court of Common Pleas, the principal *nisi prius* courts of the State, are also in session almost daily, during each of the Law School terms, while one term of the United States Circuit Court and two terms of the United States District Court are held annually in the United States Court room, not three blocks distant from the School.

THE MEDICAL DEPARTMENT.

SKETCH OF ITS HISTORY. — The Yale Medical School, situated on the west side of York Street, about midway between Chapel and Crown streets, was organized in 1812, and the first course of lectures was given in the following year. The faculty of the department numbers nine professors and eight lecturers, while the examining board consists of the faculty and an equal number of the members of the Connecticut Medical Society. The school has many important advantages, not the least of which is, that the Connecticut State Hospital, only a few blocks away, affords excellent opportunity for study of the most practical kind. To all intents and purposes this hospital is a branch of the Yale Medical School, inasmuch as it was established almost wholly through efforts of the medical faculty, and has been and is practically under their control and management. There are upwards of one hundred beds in the hospital, and students are afforded abundant opportunity to see disease in its various forms and observe the treatment of it. A morgue, where all autopsies are held, was constructed with special reference to the wants of medical classes, while an amphitheatre has been expressly provided in order that students of the Yale Medical School may witness all important surgical operations at the hospital; these operations, by the way, being performed by the professors of the school.

All candidates for admission to the Medical Department, excepting those who have passed an examination for admission to the undergraduate Academical Department of Yale College or some similar institution, must present a degree in Letters or Science from a recognized college or scientific school, or pass an examination in the following subjects :—

1. Mathematics : Algebra to Quadratics; Euclid, two books; Metric System of Weights and Measures.

2. Physics : Balfour Stewart's Elementary Physics, or any equivalent work.

THE MEDICAL SCHOOL BUILDING. — The building on York Street, occupied by the Medical Department of the University, was erected in 1860. It is a brick structure, stuccoed, and is fifty-three feet square and three stories high. As it was constructed especially for the purposes to which it is devoted, everything about it is very convenient. It contains a large, admirably lighted lecture-room, spacious and well-appointed dissecting-rooms, etc., and the museum, in which is a large collection of natural and morbid specimens, numerous casts, plates and models of elegant execution, and an extensive cabinet of materia medica. The New Haven Dispensary, located on the grounds of the Medical Department, under the management of the faculty, is visited by over six thousand patients annually. They receive the best of treatment and medicine without money and without price. Much practical benefit results to the school, however, as students are instructed in the diagnosis and treatment of the special diseases for which treatment is sought there.

THE DEPARTMENT OF THE FINE ARTS.

SKETCH OF ITS HISTORY. — "A distinct department of Fine Arts in a University, with all the appurtenances for professional art training, is a new feature in the general scheme of education which Yale College has the credit of successfully inaugurating in this country. . . . . The germ of art culture existed in the College many years ago, and Yale long enjoyed the distinction of being the first and only institution of learning in the country to establish an art collection." Fifty years ago Trumbull Gallery, now the Treasury, was erected for the display of the paintings of Colonel Trumbull. A course of lectures on art, in 1857-8, caused a renewed interest in the subject, and from that time there was a firm determination to establish a separate department devoted to it. The bountiful liberality of Mr. Augustus R. Street (Yale, 1812), of New Haven, transformed this determination from an earnest desire into a fixed fact; and to him the University is indebted for the noble edifice occupying the south-west angle of the campus, at the corner of Chapel and High streets. "He was the first to give practical expression to his conviction that the study of art comes within the scope of a great University. His aim was not simply to found a museum, but to establish a school for practical instruction for those of both sexes who are desirous of pursuing the Fine Arts as a profession, and to awake and cultivate a taste for, and appreciation of, the arts among the undergraduates and others." The great success of the Department of the Fine Arts has amply justified the wisdom of his grand idea.

YALE SCHOOL OF THE FINE ARTS.
(Page 53.)

PEABODY MUSEUM.

THE ART SCHOOL BUILDING. — In November, 1864, the corner-stone of the building was laid, and the structure was completed early in the summer of 1866. It stands on the corner of Chapel and High streets. "The architecture and construction are of what is termed revived Gothic. It consists of two wings, one 34 by 80 feet, the other 36 by 76 feet, connected by a central building 44 by 33 feet. The material used in the construction of the walls is Portland and Jersey stone, with yellow Ohio-stone ornaments. The columns of the front porch are of Gloucester polished granite, and the capitals are carved with original designs, after natural foliage, in Cleveland stone. The floors are of oak and black walnut, and the wainscotting and wood-work of chestnut. The basement contains drawing and modelling-rooms. The first story is divided into studios, class-rooms, and libraries. The second story has two large galleries lighted from the roof, for the exhibition of collections, and two wide corridors, now occupied with casts. The architect and general superintendent of the building was Mr. P. B. Wight, the architect of the National Academy of Design in New York. The expense of erecting and finishing the building amounted to about $175,000."

CONTENTS OF THE ART SCHOOL BUILDING.— The pictures were transferred to the new Art Building at once from the Trumbull Gallery, and an exhibition in 1867 of loaned works of art caused a good deal of interest to be taken in the school. Afterward a collection of casts illustrating the history of sculpture was added, and in the spring of 1868 the well-known "Jarves Collection" was temporarily placed there and subsequently became the property of the school. It is illustrative of Italian painting from the eleventh to the seventeenth centuries, and "consists of one hundred and twenty pictures, many of which are panel pictures in tempera, with gold backgrounds; others are the work of contemporary but inferior artists of the fifteenth and sixteenth centuries; and not a few are works of decided merit and great historic interest. The collection is illustrative of the rise of Christian art in Western Europe. The progress of Italian art-painting is followed, the series commencing with contemporaries of Cimabue and Giotto, continued to those of Giorgione and Veronese, illustrating the most interesting period of modern art. Many of the older pieces, principally panel paintings, are in tempera, some of which were originally designed for altar-pieces." The Jarves Gallery "contains that which is of decided value and interest to the student, who may find in it much that will enable him to grasp a fair conception of the motive which gave character to early Christian art."

OBJECTS OF THE ART SCHOOL.—The school has for its end the cultivation and promotion of the Arts of Design, viz., Painting, Sculpture and Architecture, both in their artistic and æsthetic aims, through practice and criticism. The aim is —

1st. To provide thorough technical instruction in the arts of Painting, Sculpture, and Architecture.

2d. To furnish an acquaintance with all branches of learning relating to the History, Theory, and Practice of Art.

Lectures in each department of the school are provided in addition to the technical discipline, and attendance upon these by the students is required. June 1st an exhibition of the work of the students is opened and continues through the vacation. At the close of the course prizes are offered for competition and diplomas are awarded those who pass the requisite examinations.

The school is open to both sexes, but no student will be admitted under fifteen years of age. It is open to all who desire to avail themselves of its instruction, without restrictions, save as to age and general good character. Its aim is to embrace a wide field of usefulness in connection with the knowledge and promotion of art, and to offer every facility to the student both in the way of criticism and technical discipline. The collections are open daily to the public from 1 to 5 P.M. in winter, and from 9 A.M. to 6 P.M in summer. The admission fee is small, and visitors will **be well** repaid **for spending** several hours within its walls.

As an illustration of the rapidity **of growth of the** Art Department, it **may** be stated that **in the past three years the number of** students has much more than **doubled.** Fifty-eight regular students were in attendance during the college year 1880–1. Besides these, nearly one **hundred members** of other departments received instruction in the Art **School.**

The Graduate Department.

SKETCH OF ITS HISTORY.—Graduate instruction has been a part of the work of the University from a very early date, and more especially from 1847, when measures were taken to provide courses of study for advanced students desirous of attaining a more complete knowledge of particular branches than can be obtained in a regular undergraduate course. Instruction was offered in various subjects. At first the number of students was small, but a gradual increase in number, both of students and of subjects, has taken place, until now, when the number of students is ten-fold that of 1866, and the number of subjects in which instruction is offered at present exceeds sixty, comprised in courses of Intellectual Philosophy, Political Science and History, Philological Science, Mathematics, Physics, Chemistry and Astronomy, Geology and Natural History, Applied Science, and Fine Arts. More than fifty instructors are actively connected with these courses. The Graduate Department thus far is provided with no buildings of its own, though practically it possesses several, having access to and the use of all the grand facilities of the other departments.

THE YALE SCHOOL OF JOURNALISM.—The percentage of Yale graduates engaged in the profession of journalism is larger than that of the graduates of any other American college. There are very few great journals in the country which have not, among their editors, one or more sons of Yale. This is due in a great measure, no doubt, to the course of study commonly known as the Yale School of Journalism. Technically there is no such department, the official title being the " Course of Political Science and History," in the Graduate Department, but its curriculum is so admirably adapted to the wants of the candidate for a successful career in the editorial field that it is very aptly termed by practical newspaper men " The School of Journalism." The course embraces the history of America and of Europe; relations of physical geography to political history; public finance and statistics of industry; politics and finance in the history of the United States; political economy; international law; and branches of law in general. Graduates of this and other colleges, and other persons of liberal education (not less than eighteen years old), are received as students in this department for longer or shorter periods, with or without reference to the attainment of a degree. Yale students demonstrate their practical ability in journalism by managing and editing a literary magazine of high order, two large ably-conducted bi-weeklies, and a bright, sparkling little daily, besides several carefully compiled annuals filled with all sorts of information useful to the students. -To Yale belongs the credit of establishing the first daily paper edited and managed solely by students.

Peabody Museum of Natural History,

Sketch of its History. — Peabody Museum, the north wing of which, completed in 1876, stands on the corner of High and Elm streets, was the gift of Mr. George Peabody, of London, who, in 1866, gave to certain gentlemen $150,000, in trust, for the foundation and maintenance of a museum of natural history, especially in the departments of zoology, geology, and mineralogy in connection with Yale College, in accordance, as he says in his letter conveying the offer of the gift, "with the intention I some years ago expressed of making a donation to this distinguished institution." The instrument of gift provided that of the $150,000 thus given, $100,000 was to be devoted to the erection of a fire-proof museum; $20,000 was to be invested and allowed to accumulate as a building fund until it should amount to at least $100,000, to construct one or more additions to the museum; and the balance of $30,000 was to be invested, the income from it to be used in the care of the museum and to increase the collections.

The Museum Building. — The portion of the museum already completed "was begun in 1874 and finished in 1876, and cost, including the cases, about $175,000. It has a frontage on High Street of 115 feet, and on Elm Street of 100 feet; and stands back thirty-three feet from High Street and thirty-five feet from Elm Street." When the main building and the other wing are completed, the structure will occupy the entire front on High Street, from within 33 feet of Elm Street to within that number of feet of Library Street, a distance of 344 feet; the entire lot from Elm Street to Library Street and back to a depth, from High Street, of 145 feet, having been appropriated for this purpose. A portion of the edifice will stand on a section of the land now occupied by the Gymnasium. The wing already completed is of brick, with cut-stone trimmings, has polished granite pillars at the sides of the entrance, and has three stories of 18 feet each, and a very high basement and attic, making the building as tall as one of six or seven stories of the ordinary height. Yet the visitor should bear in mind that this structure, grand as it is, is but a small portion of the edifice as it is to be when completed. "The basement is occupied by work-rooms, and contains also two large rooms which are assigned for the collection of fossil 'foot-prints.' The first story contains a large lecture-room, the mineralogical collections of the College, Professor Brush's private collections of minerals, and the mineralogical laboratory. The second story is devoted to the geological and palæontological collections, and working-rooms connected with these departments. The third story is occupied with the collections of zoology and osteology, and the appropriate laboratories of the departments of zoology and comparative anatomy. The upper story contains the collection of archæology, besides a photographic room and store-rooms." Fire-proof brick walls and iron doors separate the different portions of the building, while hose connected with iron stand-pipes is arranged at convenient points. All modern improvements in lighting, heating, and ventilating have been provided, and everything is as convenient as experience and skill can make it.

THE MINERALOGICAL COLLECTION.—The mineralogical department contains a collection of meteorites which is one of the largest in the country, and includes among its specimens a mass of meteoric iron weighing 1635 pounds. This meteorite fell in the Red River region in Texas and was brought thence to New York, via New Orleans, by a party of speculators, on the supposition that it was a mass of platinum. Thence it passed into the Lyceum of Natural

History in New York, presented to it in trust by Colonel Gibbs, of New York. "On the removal of the Lyceum from the park, it was left at the doorway, apparently forgotten. Mrs. Gibbs, the widow of Colonel Gibbs, happening to pass the spot one day, saw some workmen on the point of burying the iron in a hole they had dug ' to get it out of the way.'" She rescued it, presented it to Yale, and it now occupies a conspicuous place in the museum. It is one of the three or four largest masses of iron ever placed in a scientific museum.

THE COLLECTION OF FOSSIL REMAINS IN THE MUSEUM. — On the second floor is the very large collection of fossil remains gathered in the far West in the Yale Scientific Expeditions under the lead of Professor O. C. Marsh. When in New Haven in 1876 Professor Huxley very carefully examined the collection of vertebrate fossils in the Yale museum, and remarked of it: "I can truly and emphatically say that, so far as my knowledge extends, there is nothing in any way comparable for extent, or for the care with which the remains have been got together, or for their scientific importance, to the series of fossils which Professor Marsh has brought together." The collection in osteology brought together by Professor Marsh, to aid in the investigation of his vertebrate fossils, is believed to be the largest and most complete in this country.

THE ARCHÆOLOGICAL COLLECTION IN THE MUSEUM.— In the archæological department of the museum there are rich contributions, "consisting of about two thousand pieces of pottery, and several hundred stone implements, and many gold ornaments, which together form the most complete collection of the kind ever made."

This description gives but the merest outline of a portion of what the museum contains. Peabody Museum is open every day until 6 P.M., free to all, and visitors should, if possible, devote several hours to an examination of its contents.

READING ROOM.
(Page 29.)

TREASURY.
(Page 26.)

THE OBSERVATORY.

SKETCH OF ITS HISTORY AND WORK. — **Several** years ago, Mrs. Cornelia Hillhouse and her daughters **gave** to the University an eligibly **situated** tract **of land on** the crest of Prospect Hill, just north of Hillhouse **Avenue, as a** site for **an** observatory. In 1871-2 Hon. O. F. Winchester **made** provision for the future establishment of the proposed observatory by **the** gift of a piece of land, adjoining the site given by Mrs. Hillhouse and daughters, costing $100,000. Then **the** proposed building had not been **erected, but was to be in due time.** Meanwhile, the work of the **Observatory had begun by the** establishment of **a** public time service and **a thermometric** bureau. **By a** contract with the State, the **College daily** transmits the exact time **to every railroad** station in Connecticut, the standard of time adopted being **that** now officially known as Eastern. The action of Connecticut **in** establishing a time service is the first of its kind in the country, **and was** made possible by the excellent facilities afforded by the Observatory of Yale College. As to the thermometric bureau, it also is of great public benefit. Up to June, 1881, it had issued no less than 1,957 certificates for thermometers sent there to be tested, "the larger portion of which numerically has been of clinical thermometers designed for use by physicians. The great errors which **have been** found in many **of these** instruments show that the work **which the bureau** is doing **is a real service to** the people. Some of **the thermometers examined and verified have been** of unusual accuracy or peculiar construction. Those needed for use in the Arctic explorations undertaken by the United States Signal Service may be specially mentioned.

OBSERVATORY BUILDING. — The Observatory Building, erected in 1883, stands on the crest of Prospect Hill. The tower is circular and is arranged with all the most approved machinery for rapid and easy manipulation. Connected is a substantial large square, brick house, suitable for a dwelling for the official in charge and for laboratories required in various parts of the work to which the observatory is devoted. A few rods distant from the main building is a second tower, identical in outward appearance with that attached to the house.

EQUIPMENT OF THE OBSERVATORY. — The equipment now in use consists in part of: —

1. An Astronomical Observatory, inclusive of standard clocks, transit instruments, chronographs, and the accessories for refined accuracy in the determination and transmission of time.

2. A complete apparatus for the testing of chronometers, watches, and clocks in the various positions and conditions of temperature, arranged with reference to the safety against fire and theft of such instruments while in the care of the observatory.

3. The apparatus for an extended (automatic) public time service.

4. The apparatus for research and comparison in Thermometry, including comparators, cathetometers, and a collection of the best thermometers obtainable of the foreign makers and observatories which devote special attention to thermometric standards.

5. A heliometer completed late in 1881 by Messrs. Repsold, of Hamburg. This instrument, which required eighteen months in construction, is the largest and finest heliometer in the world, and cost about $7,200.

ATHLETIC INTERESTS, CLUBS, AND THE FENCE.

THE **YALE ATHLETIC** GROUNDS.—The Yale Athletic Grounds, a beautifully situated tract comprising about thirty acres of land, lie on the west bank of West River, on the southern side of Derby Avenue, a little over a mile from the college campus. Derby **Avenue** is a branch of West Chapel Street, and horse-cars, passing the College every twelve minutes, go within a short walk of the field. The greater portion of the land lies **on a bluff,** thirty feet **above the river, and looks in one** direction toward **the harbor, and in another toward the city,** while on the western side lies **Edgewood Hill. In the fourth direction** is an excellent view of **West Rock. On the whole, it is** difficult **to see** how a more beautiful situation **could have been** obtained. It is designed to have within the grounds **a place for** every field-sport the students are likely to care for, including several base-ball grounds, cricket, foot-ball **and** polo grounds, lawn-tennis courts, a large field for athletic exhibitions, race-track, etc., **etc., on the** main field, and a rifle-range under the bluff, **on the bank of** the river. Although **the land was not purchased until the spring of 1881,** considerable work had **been** done before the close **of** the following summer, under direction of the committee having the matter in charge, by whom plans were **obtained before** Commencement. **These plans** contemplate what will **be, when completed, altogether** the largest, most convenient and beautiful **grounds for athletic sports in America,** or in fact, in the world. **Among the buildings will be a residence for the** keeper, at least two edifices **fitted up with** bath-rooms, dressing-rooms and other conveniences, and a large grand stand so built as to face in two directions. There are two beautiful large pines at the main entrance, and lovely drives will be laid out all through the grounds, considerable portions of which will be shaded by trees planted for the purpose. There is already a handsome chestnut grove on the bluff, just above the river. Of course all these improvements will require considerable time for completion, from the nature of things, but the work is going on as rapidly and steadily as is consistent with the best results. The cost of the land was about $21,000, and the improvements will cost from $10,000 to $20,000 more. The money is subscribed mostly by graduates and students of Yale.

HAMILTON PARK. — Hamilton Park, located about a mile and three-quarters from the University, is accessible by the Westville horse-cars, these vehicles passing directly by the main entrance, which is on Whalley Avenue. The park is a very large, level tract of land, surrounded by a high board fence. An excellent half-mile track occupies a portion of the space, and it is in the southern half of the ellipse formed by this track that practically all the important base-ball and foot-ball games in New Haven, between the representatives of Yale and those of other colleges, have been played. On this field Yale has won many of her most brilliant triumphs. Here was witnessed the famous 5 to 0 game with Harvard, in base-ball, and on these grounds Thompson kicked the goal which gave Yale the foot-ball championship over Harvard away back in 1876, and which Yale has held uninterruptedly to the present time. In base-ball at Hamilton Park between Yale and Harvard, of eight University games Yale has won six and Harvard two; and of the five class games played there between Yale and Harvard, Yale has won all. At the close of the base-ball season of 1881, there had been sixty-four games of base-ball between the University and class nines of Yale and those of Harvard, since 1866 (when the first game was played), of which Yale won 35 and Harvard 29. Of the total of perhaps twenty-five base-ball games played since 1876, between Yale and other colleges than Harvard, Yale won twenty. For the six successive years ending with the season of 1884, Yale has held the championship in base-ball over all other colleges. In 1880 this result was secured by defeating Princeton, after the latter had beaten all other nines. Of eight college games in that year Yale won seven and lost one. In 1881 Yale won seven college games and lost three, Harvard and Princeton coming second with six games won and four lost, each. The result was exceedingly gratifying to Yale from the fact that every one of her opponents — Amherst, Brown, Dartmouth, Harvard and Princeton — had a nine capable of contesting the supremacy with almost any professional club in the country.

On Hamilton Park Yale has played several important games of foot-ball. Since 1876, when the present custom of playing by the Rugby rules was adopted, Yale has never lost a game on this field, though her representatives have on numerous occasions met there and played with teams from Harvard, Amherst, Columbia, Trinity, Rutgers and other colleges. In 1876, the Yale University foot-ball team met and defeated the Harvard University team, one goal to nothing; in 1877, no game was played; in 1878, Yale met and defeated the Harvard University team at Boston, one goal to nothing; in 1879, the game at New Haven was a draw, neither side winning a goal; in 1880, Yale met and defeated the Harvard University team at Boston, one goal to nothing; and in 1881, at New Haven, Yale was again victorious, having compelled Harvard to make four safety-touchdowns to nothing. And so on down to the close of the season of 1884, Yale has uninterruptedly held the University championship over Harvard at foot-ball; and in all the University games she has played in foot-ball with college opponents, under the Rugby rules, Yale has lost but two goals — a record equalled by no other similar organization, amateur or professional, in the world. The Yale University foot-ball team at present holds the championship over all college teams in America, having won, in the last complete series played, one more game than any other team in the league.   In class games of foot-ball, also, Yale has been very successful, having won from Harvard since the first class game under the present rules in '76, eight games and lost two.   Thus of the total of nineteen games played between Yale and Harvard, Yale has won fifteen, Harvard has won three, and one game has been a draw.

THE BOAT-HOUSE. — The Yale Boat-House, on the Chapel Street bridge, a short distance below East Street, is well worth a visit from those who take an interest in aquatic sports.   The building stands on rows of piles driven into the bed of the stream, and is 83 by 75 feet in size.   It resembles closely the boat-house of the London Rowing Club.   Practically the entire first floor is occupied as a store-room for the boats, oars, rowing tackle, etc., though a small portion of the space is used by the boat carpenter in making repairs.   The boats, of which there are scores, are suspended from arms attached to the posts sustaining the second floor, and are arranged in tiers one above another.   Almost every variety of light craft is found here, from the genuine Indian canoe to the paper shell used in the University race with Harvard.   Passing along between the tiers of boats to the west side of the room five large doors are reached, from which very broad gang-planks lead to the float — a wooden platform rising and falling with the tide.   When it is desired to launch a boat the men who are to use it take it from its station in the boat-house, carry it — for all the boats are very light — down to the float, place it in the water and step aboard.   The second story contains a hall, the walls of which are decorated with the pictures and names of several prominent promoters of Yale's boating interests.   This floor also contains an office and a large room or suite of rooms filled with lockers or closets for the oarsmen.   Bath-rooms, dressing-rooms, etc., are attached.   A broad veranda surrounds the second story and affords a delightful position from which to view those practising in the boats.   The boat-house is open every day during term-time.   Visitors are perfectly welcome.

The boat-house was built in the spring of 1875, at a cost, including the land, of about $16,500. June 9, 1875, it was formally dedicated, the ceremonies including speeches by President Porter, Rev. Joseph H. Twichell, Professor Brewer and Mr. W. C. Gulliver. A grand ball in the evening closed the festivities.

Among other objects of interest, the Yale boat-house contains the three eight-oar shells in which the Yale University Crew won its triumphs over the Harvard University Crew in the annual races of 1876, 1880 and 1881. The first eight-oar straight-away race between the Yale and Harvard crews was rowed at Springfield, Mass., in 1876. Yale won. In 1877 the race was rowed at the same place, and Harvard won. The seven remaining races, up to and including that of 1884, were rowed on the Thames at New London, Conn., of which Yale won three and Harvard four; Harvard winning those of '78, '79, '82 and '83, and Yale those of 1880, '81 and '84. The Yale crew of 1880 and 1881 is universally conceded to have been the tallest, heaviest, and most powerful eight, either professional or amateur, that ever sat in a boat. The men averaged about six feet in height, weighed 176 pounds each, and had an average age, in 1881, of about 22½ years. The Yale crew of 1876 was lighter, but exceedingly skilful, and from its numbers, after winning the University race from Harvard, was chosen the Yale Centennial Four which won a world-wide fame by its brilliant victories at Philadelphia in the summer of that year.

Previous to 1876, in the races where several colleges, including Yale and Harvard, had crews, Yale won one and Harvard none. The race won by Yale was one of the most extensive in point of numbers of colleges represented, ever rowed in America, eleven crews having been engaged in the contest. Of the two single-scull races rowed between representatives of Yale and Harvard, as such, Yale won both.

Since 1852, up to and including 1884, representatives of Yale and Harvard, as such, have met in friendly rivalry on the water thirty-eight times, of which Yale has crossed the line ahead seventeen times and Harvard twenty-one times. Twice when Yale has come in ahead Harvard has received the nominal victory on the claim of a foul, the real victory remaining with **Yale.** **As will be** seen above, up to and including **1884,** nine eight-oar races had **been rowed** between the University **crews of Yale and Harvard,** of which **Yale** won four and Harvard five.

SUMMARY OF BASE-BALL, BOATING AND FOOT-BALL.— In 1852 Yale and Harvard met in friendly rivalry in **college sports for** the first time. Since that year, up to and including the year 1884, representatives of the two colleges have contended for the supremacy in the three great college sports, base-ball, boating and foot-ball, a total of one hundred and forty-two times, in which Yale has been victorious eighty-one **times, Harvard** sixty times, and there has been one draw. For convenience of reference the following table, compiled from the facts in the two **preceding articles, is given :—**

	Yale won.	Harvard won.
Base-ball,	51	34
Boating,	15	23
Foot-ball,	15	3
	81	60

Total **of** decisive contests between **Yale** and Harvard,   . **141**
Yale victorious over Harvard, ... **81 times.**
Harvard victorious over Yale, ... 60 "

THE **YALE** UNIVERSITY **CLUB.**— One of the most interesting **of the more recent** institutions connected with the University is the Yale University Club. **For** some **time** previous to **June, 1880,** there had been some talk of organizing a club different **from anything in New Haven, but no definite action had been taken.** In that month, however, about twenty-five men from the class of **1881, and** as many more from the **class of 1882, met, discussed** the project, appointed a committee **to look into details, etc., and the** result was the formal

LIBRARY.
(Page 27.)

STUDENT'S ROOM IN DURFEE.
(Page 23.)

organization of the Yale University Club, which has since become incorporated. Undergraduates at once subscribed about $1,600, while more than a hundred graduates became honorary members and added funds to the treasury. During the vacation of 1880, a lease, with privilege of purchase, was obtained of the large three-story brick, stuccoed front, house at No. 438 Chapel Street, immediately below the New Haven House and facing the Green. In the course of the summer the building was re-fitted and re-furnished at an expense of $2,000, making the place a most inviting one. On the first floor front is the restaurant, and in the rear is an office where writing materials are furnished for the use of members of the club. On the second floor is a large and pleasant reading-room, overlooking the Green, with open fire, papers, magazines, etc. This is the general meeting-room. The two remaining rooms on this floor are for private clubs. On the third floor are four rooms used for the same purpose. The yard in the rear of the building serves as a lawn tennis court. Membership in the club is confined to the two upper classes in the Academical Department and the upper class in the Scientific Department, and to graduates. The club is chiefly valued for its social advantages, as it gives men in the two upper classes an opportunity for a freer and better intercourse than seniors and juniors have hitherto enjoyed. A second object is to bring the graduates and undergraduates into communication, and a third is to furnish a sort of headquarters for Yale men in and out of New Haven, where they can meet and consult. In short it is to draw closer the bonds which unite all members of the great Yale family, gradually extending its limits as room and means permit.

THE FENCE.— The visitor to Yale could hardly lay claim to having seen all the objects of interest were he to depart without viewing the widely renowned and ever popular "Fence." The memory of the "oldest living graduate" runneth not back to the time when the fence surrounding the Yale campus first became popular as a rendezvous for students. An old graduate states incidentally in a letter that nearly half a century ago he and several companions decided to establish the Yale Literary Magazine, one evening " while sitting on the fence." And what is this fence ? Simply a three-railed, wooden structure, the rails being round and about four inches in diameter, the upper rail affording a good seat and the middle one a convenient place on which to rest the feet. " The Fence " proper is that portion on the corner of Chapel and College streets which extends from the corner westward on Chapel Street to South College and northward on College Street a distance of perhaps 300 feet. Here on every pleasant evening hundreds of students gather, the seniors occupying the portion of the fence on Chapel Street from South College down to the first gate, the juniors the portion from that gate to the corner of College Street, and the sophomores the portion on College Street from the corner to the first gate. By college custom, which is more faithfully obeyed than any statute ever framed, no freshman is allowed to sit on the fence until the freshman base-ball nine has defeated the Harvard freshman base-ball nine in a match game. These games do not occur until quite near the close of freshman year, yet so zealously coveted is the honor of sitting on the fence for even that short period, that but two classes have failed, during fifteen years, to beat the Harvard freshmen at base-ball. After "winning the fence," the freshmen are at perfect liberty to occupy their section of it, from the first gate on College Street northward as much as they choose without molestation from anyone. A sophomore would never think of sitting on the junior fence nor a junior on the senior fence — in other words, no under-classman ever sits on the fence of an upper-classman, but an upper-classman may sit on the fence of any class below him. About a week before Commencement a sophomore, selected for the occasion, delivers a humorous speech, resigning the sophomore fence to the freshmen about to become sophomores. A freshman always attempts to reply, but his voice is drowned by shouts of the hundreds of upper-classmen who have gathered around him. Just previous to this ceremony the three upper classes have, headed by a band, marched in procession all through the campus, and the streets are lined with ladies and gentlemen gathered to witness the affair. On ordinary occasions, while sitting on the fence, the classes sing college songs, tell stories and plan all sorts of things. Whenever anything of importance has happened, a grand rush is made for the fence, where particulars are always first obtained. But "The Fence" is as dear to the graduate as to the undergraduate, and in Commencement week if an alumnus who has returned to the scenes of his college days desires to find his classmates, he straightway turns his footsteps toward the corner of Chapel and College streets, where he is sure to discover his cronies assembled, as in days of yore, "On the Fence." Once there he is perfectly happy,

> "Nor other home, nor other care intends;
> But quits his house, his country and his friends."

COMMENCEMENT, AND OTHER FESTIVALS.

COMMENCEMENT WEEK.— So many visitors are present in New Haven during Commencement Week, and on various other public occasions, that it may not be inappropriate to give a brief outline of the exercises generally pursued at those times. Commencement Day at Yale occurs on the last Wednesday in June, annually, and Commencement Week is the week ending on Commencement Day. On Friday preceding Commencement Day ten members of the senior class compete for the De Forest prize medal, valued at $100, awarded "to that scholar of the class who shall write and pronounce an English oration in the best manner." The exercises occur in Battell Chapel. On the forenoon of the following Sunday, at 10.30, the President delivers the baccalaureate sermon at Battell Chapel. The next day, Monday, is Presentation Day, more familiarly known among the students as Class-Day. At 10.30 A.M. the members of the senior class of the Academical Department form in procession near the Old Chapel and march thence to Battell Chapel, where the exercises consist of singing, the reading of a poem by the class poet and the delivery of an address by the class orator, at the close of which a list of the successful contestants for various prizes is read by the President. In the afternoon, at 2 o'clock, the senior class assembles within an immense amphitheatre of seats constructed specially for the occasion on the campus, in front of South Middle College. The raised seats, capable of accommodating several thousand persons, are filled with fair friends of the class, while the students themselves sit on benches arranged for the purpose within the circle. The exercises open with the passing around of very long-stemmed pipes, which may be filled from great bucketsful of fine-cut tobacco prepared for the purpose. Lemonade in abundance completes the outfit. Programmes are distributed, a song or two is sung, and then the class historians, of whom there are four or five, take turns in reading the "history" of the class and of its individual members. Generally the wittiest men in the class are chosen for these positions, and the result is that the entire audience is kept in an almost continual roar of laughter at the jokes perpetrated on the various members of the class. At the completion of these exercises, the class forms in procession, and, headed by a band, marches to some chosen spot beside one of the stone buildings on the campus, and plants the class ivy; a brief ceremony, which is quite touching. Again forming in line the procession marches to the residences of the President and the older professors, saluting them with cheers. Returning to the campus, the class cheers the various buildings, and, at dusk, breaks ranks for the last time as a class.

On Tuesday of Commencement Week the Society of the Alumni holds its anniversary at Alumni Hall, when the state of the College is discussed and business matters in reference thereto taken into consideration. Speeches are indulged in to a considerable extent. On the same day occurs the anniversary of the Scientific Department at Sheffield Hall, and of the Law Department at the Law School Building, at which there is speaking, award of prizes, etc., and a general good time. It is usually intended to have one or more excellent speakers present, so that the visitor is sure of a rare treat.

COMMENCEMENT DAY.— Commencement Day is the most interesting and important of any in the college calendar. As early as 1717 it became a public festival, and from that time to the present has ever been looked forward to with great pleasure, in each succeeding year, by graduates and undergraduates, clergy and laymen, faculty and

students, mothers, brothers, sisters and friends. On that day hundreds
of ladies and gentlemen, gathered from all parts of the country, are
present in the beautiful "City of Elms" to witness the graduation of
sons and brothers, cousins and lovers. Wealth, beauty, culture and
refinement are all largely represented. An entire stranger to the city
and to the College would recognize at once by the remarkable animation
and general holiday air that the day was one of unusual importance.
Shortly after 9 o'clock in the forenoon all the graduates who happen
to be in town assemble on the campus, near the corner of Chapel and
College streets, where a procession is formed, consisting of the President and distinguished guests, graduates in the order of graduation,
graduates of other colleges, and the graduating classes, in the order
here given. The procession marches out through the Chapel Street
gate, moves along College Street to the Old State House entrance to
New Haven Green, and thence to Centre Church, where Commencement exercises are held. Here the procession files into the church
between lines of undergraduates drawn up on either side of the
entrance, and takes seats that have been reserved for it near the centre
aisle. Meanwhile the spacious edifice has filled with the friends of the
College and of the graduating classes, admission having been gained
by tickets distributed among those about to graduate and by them
given to their friends. Every available seat is occupied. Generations
ago, the custom was adopted of seating the members of the fair sex
upon one side of the church and their sterner companions on the
other, at Yale commencements. Tradition has it that this method was
seized upon as an expedient to stop whispering while the speaking
was in progress. Whatever the motive, the result has been a much
more quiet state of affairs during the exercises than was enjoyed previous to the adoption of the plan, which has been quite consistently
adhered to even to the present day. The above explanation will make
clear to the visitor what might otherwise seem very peculiar to him
upon entering Centre Church on Commencement Day. The exercises
at the church consist of prayer and music, the delivery of the valedictory

SHEFFIELD HALL.
(Page 40.)

NORTH SHEFFIELD HALL.

and salutatory addresses, and speaking by ten of the best orators in the graduating class. As a general thing, the last speaker closes at about 1 o'clock P.M., when the graduating class, having been formed two abreast, just outside the entrance, marches up to and upon the platform, in squads of a dozen or fifteen, and there receives from the hand of the President, rolls of degrees, which are assorted after the squads have passed down and out of the church. The presentation of the degrees is accompanied by a very brief address in Latin from the President. Immediately after the last degree has been conferred the exercises are brought to a close by singing and the benediction.

The ringing of the Centre Church bell at the conclusion of the literary exercises warns the graduates, young and old, to wend their way, in company with their special guests, to Alumni Hall, where a substantial repast has been prepared. Speeches follow the dinner, and evening is fast approaching ere the assemblage finally and reluctantly takes its departure.

In the evening, the President holds a reception at the School of the Fine Arts, when it is customary for all who attend to do so in full evening dress. The halls and galleries of the spacious edifice are always filled to their utmost capacity on these occasions. The reception usually continues from 8 o'clock until 10 o'clock, and with its close terminates Commencement.

JUNIOR EXHIBITION.— Junior Exhibition, an institution extending back many years, occurs annually on the Thursday next preceding the spring recess, this recess beginning usually on the Wednesday preceding Easter. Several weeks previous to that time all members of the junior class of the Academical Department having a certain rank are required to write an essay on any one of perhaps eight subjects provided by the professor of rhetoric. The writers of the ten best essays are afterward chosen to declaim their productions in public. The occasion on which the declamations take place is known as the Junior Exhibition, or more familiarly, "Junior Ex." It occurs on the day mentioned above, in the Battell Chapel at 2 o'clock P.M., and is quite fully attended, the audience generally containing quite a number of visitors from other cities. Taking the first prize is considered the greatest honor of junior year.

JUNIOR PROMENADE.— The most important social event of the year is the Junior Promenade, which occurs in the second term, just previous to Lent. It is gotten up in the most elegant manner, by a committee of the leading society men of the junior class appointed especially for that purpose. Neither pains nor expense are spared. Even the minutest details receive the utmost care. Elegant cards of invitation are issued, on which appears the class numeral disposed with great taste, while the order of dances, etc., displays the highest skill of the "art preservative." Carll's Opera House is the scene of the festivities, which are attended by fashion and beauty from all sections of the country. No event of the kind, anywhere, excels the magnificence of the Junior Promenade at Yale, and no college event, except Commencement, attracts so large an attendance of visitors. The influx is very noticeable about the College for two or three days previous to the Promenade, and the most casual observer cannot but notice the air of festivity which prevails. Many of those who have come for the purpose of being present at the Promenade attend college prayers, during their stay, at Battell Chapel, occupying the spacious galleries.

SENIOR PROMENADE.— The Senior Promenade, occurring on the evening of the Monday preceding Commencement, ranks with the leading social events of college life at Yale. Like the Junior Promenade, it is carried out in elegant style, and enjoys as its guests the beauty and refinement of the land. For years it was held at Alumni Hall, when the campus was lighted up with a profusion of Chinese lanterns, presenting a weird but very attractive spectacle. Henceforward these Promenades will occur at Carll's Opera House, opposite the college grounds, on Chapel Street.

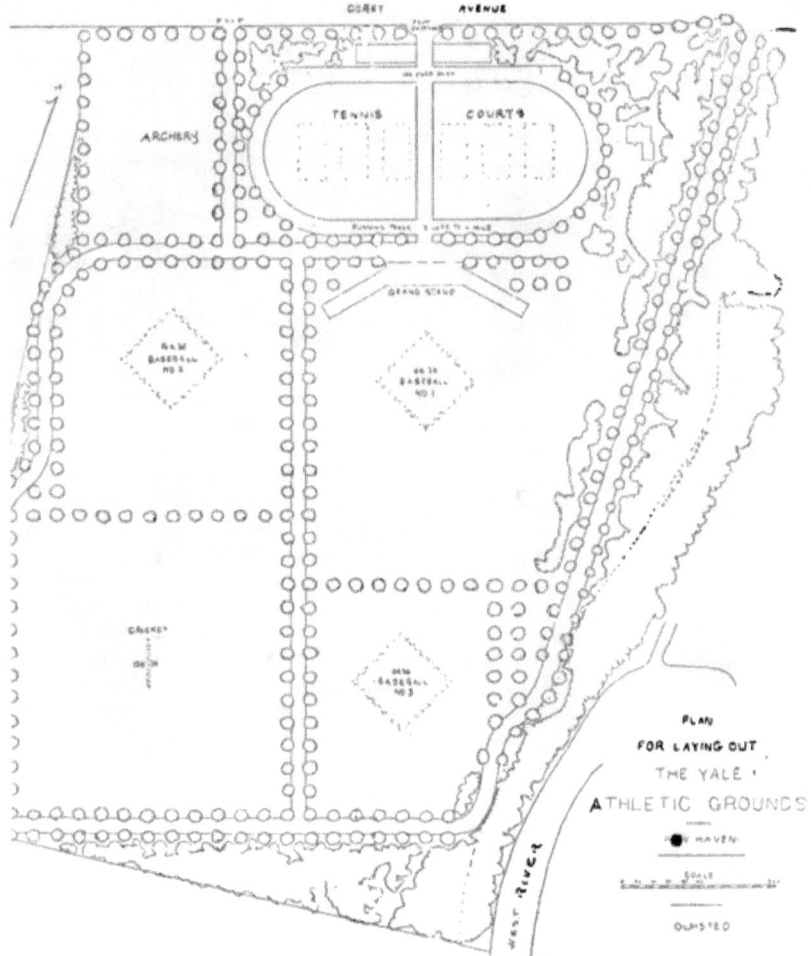

PLAN
FOR LAYING OUT
THE YALE
ATHLETIC GROUNDS
NEW HAVEN

SCALE

OLMSTED

"The City of Elms:"

New Haven, Connecticut.

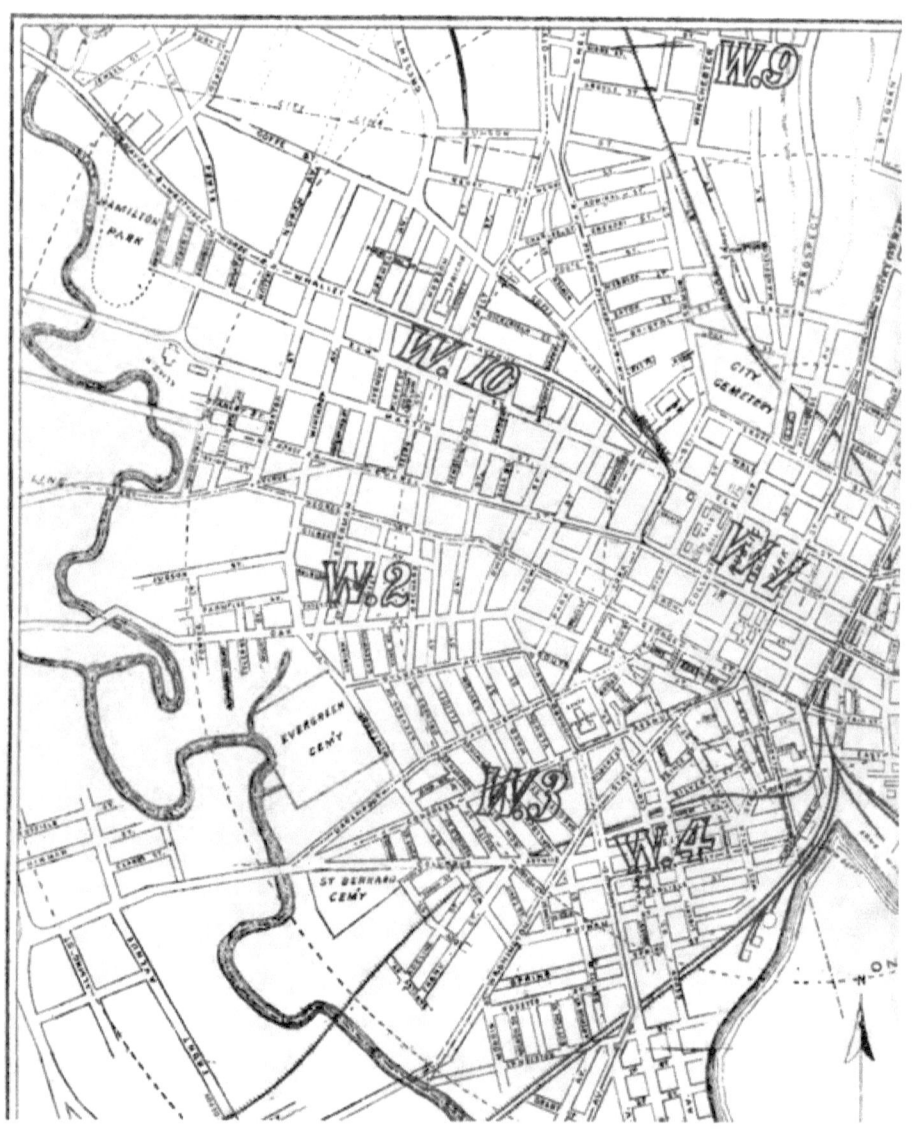

MAP OF
NEW HAVEN

HISTORY IN BRIEF.

NEW HAVEN, **the home of** the distinguished University described in the preceding pages, **lies** at the head of New Haven Bay, Connecticut, on an alluvial **plain four miles from** Long Island Sound, and seventy-three **miles from New York City.** The land in the portions thus far **built upon, is** quite level, terminating very abruptly in a range of trap-**dikes,** the two highest points in which are known as West Rock and **East** Rock, respectively. The site of the city **was once,** long ages ago, **the** mouth of the Connecticut River. The formation of the trap-dikes and ridges, of which East and West Rocks are a part, formed an impassi-**ble** barrier, however, and "in this extremity the river," **as** Prof. James **D.** Dana says, "finding a way to the south-eastward **open** before it, made a rush through **the narrows at Middletown and was off for Say-**brook, leaving New Haven in the **lurch.** Perhaps, after all, New Haven is none the worse for the loss. **If New** Haven Bay were now the mouth **of the** Connecticut, the fair plain, the site of the city and its surrounding **villages, would be swept by floods** and tides, and build-ing places would be confined to **the** slopes and tops of **the Rocks and** other hills. **New** Haven **has balanced the** account with **Saybrook by taking from** her Yale **College; and we** think she has **double reason to** be content with the **change."**

New Haven was founded in 1638 by a party of Puritans under John Davenport, who **had been forced to leave** England in 1637, and had, after remaining at **Boston nearly a year,** continued their travels to the **site of the present New Haven, then** known as Quinnipiac. The "most opulent colony which came into New England," its members, under Davenport's direction, immediately laid out a portion of the land into nine squares for buildings, reserving the large central square for public uses. The boundaries of the land thus portioned off into squares are the present York, State, Grove and George streets, and the first dwellings were erected on or near George Street, between Church and College streets. For many years the colony was governed by its seven most distinguished church members, Davenport, by virtue of his intelligence, uprightness and natural ability as a leader, continuing at the head. From the first, when they bought the land of the Quinni-piac Indians for "12 coats of English cloth, 12 alchymy spoons, 12 hatchets, 12 hoes, 2 dozen knives, 12 porringers and 4 cases of French knives and scissors," the New Haven colonists seem to have been great traders, and trading posts were early established at various points on the Delaware. These were broken up by the Swedes, whereupon many of the settlers, becoming discouraged, determined to sail in 1647, to Gal-loway, Ireland. The ship was never heard from, though there is a tradi-tion that upon a day months after the departure, the craft sailed into New Haven harbor, in the face of the wind, and suddenly, when near the wharf, vanished into thin air. The myth has been beautifully put in verse by Longfellow in his "Phantom Ship." In 1665 New Haven Plantation united with Connecticut (Hartford) Plantation, on the condi-tion that each town should remain a capital. Thus it happened that for over two centuries, or until within a very few years of the present time, Connecticut had two capitals; one at Hartford, the other at New Haven. Indian wars for some time gave the New Haveners much trouble, while the Revolution caused an almost infinite amount of privation, distress and sorrow. From here marched Benedict Arnold to Cam-bridge in 1775 with the Governor's Guards, reputed to have been the best company in the American army; and here Washington reviewed the troops while on his way to take the position of Commander-in-Chief at Cambridge. At sunrise, July 5th, 1779, about two thousand Hessians and Tories landed on the West Haven shore, four miles from

EAST DIVINITY HALL.
(Page 44.)

New Haven. **Their march** to the town was very much impeded by Yale students, **headed by President Daggett,** and by townsmen and militia, who contested every inch of ground. President Daggett was, among others, captured with **gun in hand, and taken to town as a prisoner.** New Haven was **pillaged,** and, in part, destroyed by fire. It was some years before the **effects of this blow were entirely recov-**ered from. With the dawn of better days, **New Haven, incorporated** a city in 1784, entered upon a career of remarkable prosperity, which has continued almost uninterrupted to the present time. **Very few are** the cities, anywhere, **that have grown so** steadily and continued so rapidly to **increase in wealth and population. In 1820 the number of inhabitants was but 8,326, while** in 1860 it had increased to 39,268; **in 1870 to 50,840; in 1880 to 62,882; and in the fall of** 1881 it prob-**ably very** closely approached to 65,000. In size, New Haven ranks third among New England cities, Boston and Providence, only, exceed-**ing it.** To a considerable degree this success is due to manufacturing, which is carried on to a great extent **and** in almost every conceivable **variety.** For years New Haven was **one of the leading cities in the world in** the manufacture of carriages; **and to-day an immense num-ber of** vehicles of **the very finest description** are turned **out, and find** their **way** to all the countries of the **globe.** Fire-arms **of the most** approved patterns, clocks, locks and fish-lines, paper boxes and knick-knacks of **all kinds** are annually manufactured at New Haven **by** millions. **Pianos, organs,** rubber boots and shoes, corsets, scales, hay-cutters, etc., are **also produced in New Haven** in great quantity. **It is** a fact that, let **one go where he will, in the** "City of Elms" he is **quite sure to find all available space in the** rear of stores **and dwell-ings occupied by factories, each of which** is a bee-hive of industry. **A large pork-packing industry and** an extensive West India trade, also, **are carried on. As would be expected of** a city so **prosperous in trade and manufacture,** its business houses include many **structures of the largest size, filled with** goods of the very best quality **and descrip-tion. An air of thrift pervades** them all, from the great **wholesale** houses on State Street, to the less pretentious retail up-town stores. The stranger needs to remain in New Haven but a very short time to discover that he is in a very lively, bright and wide-awake New England city.

But hand in hand with material prosperity and growth, in the "City of Elms," have gone an intellectual growth and a continued social advance, so that in no city in the world are the people more generally or highly educated, or the tone of society better. The colonists who settled here were eminently intelligent, clear-minded persons, appreciating fully the great advantages of refinement and education. Almost their first act after forming a church was the establishment of a school. Yale College is one of the great results of their policy. Descended from so worthy an ancestry, the community of to-day could not be other than the highly cultivated, vigorous one that it is.

And what of New Haven's general appearance? It is unquestionably one of the most beautiful cities in the world, and one which the stranger always remembers with pleasure. Nowhere else can be found the wealth of broad-spreading, shadow-casting elms possessed by New Haven. Its appellation, the "City of Elms," is well applied. Street after street, avenue after avenue, is arched with these noble trees. As to beauty and variety of architecture displayed in the dwellings, nothing, anywhere, excels it. A vast majority of the houses are of wood, while no two, scarcely, are alike. Every style and shape seem to have been brought into requisition. As a rule, the residences have more or less lawn and yard room, the habit of crowding the buildings thickly together, so often seen in a large city, being conspicuously absent. The streets, as a general thing, are broad and straight, and in most cases cross one another at right angles. In this respect New Haven clearly resembles Philadelphia, which, however, it much preceded in the use of this method, inasmuch as the original nine squares of which New Haven was composed, were laid out long years before William Penn founded the "City of Brotherly Love." Like Philadelphia too, New Haven has several beautiful public parks or greens, appearing here and there about the city, like grass-plats in a garden. Willis's description of the city's appearance, though written a number of years ago, and as he recollected seeing it in his college days, still applies well, in a general way, and will bear reproduction at this time :—

"If you were to set a poet to make a town, with *carte blanche* as to trees, gardens and green blinds, he would probably turn out very much such a place as New Haven. The first thought of the inventor of New Haven was to lay out the streets in parallelograms; the second was to plant them from suburb to water-side, with the magnificent elms of the country. The result is that, at the end of fifty years, the town is buried in leaves. If it were not for the spires of the churches, a bird flying over on his autumn voyage to the Floridas would never mention having seen it in his travels. The houses are something between an Italian palace and an English cottage,—built of wood, but, in the dim light of those overshadowing trees, as fair to the eye as marble, with their triennial coats of paint; and each stands in the midst of its own encircling grass-plot, half buried in vines and flowers, and facing outward from a cluster of gardens divided by slender palings, and filling up with fruit trees and summer-houses the square on whose limit it stands. Then, like the vari-colored parallelograms upon a chess-board, green openings are left throughout the town, fringed with triple and interweaving elm rows, the long weeping branches sweeping downward to the grass, and, with their inclosing shadows, keeping moist and cool the road they overhang."

Concerning the scenery about New Haven, it is, as Professor Beers has well said, "uncommonly rich and varied, tempting constantly to holiday walks and sails, and lending a romantic charm to the memories of undergraduate life. There is an intimate blending of sea-side and inland. Brackish creeks empty and fill their sluices with tide-water, at the bases of cliffs miles from the sea. Following a path through woods, you come **out suddenly on the borders** of a salt **marsh,** where **gulls are flying about.   Lying under the trees** of an orchard seemingly **in the heart of the continent, you lift** your eyes and see across the **clover-tops the sparkle of the sun on the** waters of the Sound, and the **sail of a vessel bound for New York.   You could** put out your hand **and touch it,** lying **under** the apple-trees."

Thus much for New Haven in general.   **Now for a few hints to the** visitor, and brief descriptions of various objects of interest **about the** city.   In the first place, the visitor will probably arrive either **by cars, or by** steamboat from New York.   The hotels may be reached **by horse cars** or coaches, **from** the New Haven line of steamboats or **from the** Union depot, **at which all** trains, except those of the Derby road, **stop.   Coaches are the means of conveyance** from the wharf of the Starin **Line of steamboats.**

Fares in the public carriages or **coaches from any railroad station or** steamboat dock to **any point within the city limits, are fifty cents for** one passenger, seventy-five cents for **two passengers destined for the** same point; and for each additional **passenger, more than two, like-wise destined, twenty-five cents.   Children over four and under ten** years of age, one-half the above rates.   Each passenger is entitled at these rates, which are established by law, to the carriage of one trunk and valise or other similar article.   In the horse cars the fare is five cents on the lines running from the depot to the principal thorough-fare,—Chapel Street,—and six cents on all other lines.   By purchasing **a** transfer check, price eight cents, on the single car in front **of the** Union depot, the visitor may secure a ride to within a few rods of any of the principal hotels, **which** are the New Haven House, the Elliott House, the Tontine Hotel and the Tremont House, ranking **in the** order named.   The New Haven House is one of **the best** managed hotels in America, and is first-class in every respect.

The visitor will find that most of **the principal points** of interest beyond easy walking distance of **the hotels may** be reached by horse cars.   **For** points in Fair Haven and the eastern section of the city, the Fair Haven and Westville Line should be taken (cars run every twelve minutes); also the same line for Westville, West Rock, Edgewood and other points in a westerly direction; for State Street, East Rock and other points in a north-easterly direction, the State Street Line (cars run every twelve minutes); for Whitney Avenue, Whitneyville, Whitney Lake, etc., the Whitney Avenue Line (cars run every half hour); for Congress and Sylvan avenues, Evergreen Cemetery, the State Hospital and points in a south-westerly direction, the Congress Avenue Line (cars run every twenty minutes); for West Haven, Savin Rock and the West Shore, the New Haven and West Haven Line (cars run every fifteen minutes in summer, every half hour in other seasons); for the Winchester Arms Works and Newhallville, the Shelton Avenue Line (cars run every thirteen minutes). Cars on all these lines, except the Shelton Avenue Line, may be taken at the corner of Chapel and Church streets. The starting point for the cars of the Shelton Avenue Line is the corner of York Street and Broadway.

For the sake of convenience the city has been divided, in the descriptions which follow, into four sections, which may be denominated, in a general way, Northern, Southern, Eastern and Western New Haven, respectively. The intersection of Chapel and Church streets being near the centre of the city, and also being the meeting place of several horse-car lines, has been chosen as a point of departure for the various tours that follow.

Northern New Haven.

GENERAL DESCRIPTION. — Northern New Haven is to a considerable degree a district filled with noble mansions and large, costly estates, bordering on streets and avenues of at least unexcelled, not to say unrivalled, beauty. To friends of Yale, this portion of the city will have an additional charm, from the fact that here have lived many of the greatest benefactors of and instructors in the University. And to-day a very considerable proportion of the professors and instructors have their homes here.

TEMPLE STREET AND THE GREEN. — Taking the corner of Church and Chapel streets as a point of departure and passing west on Chapel Street one block or square, the visitor reaches Temple Street, declared by an eminent writer to be the most beautiful highway in the world. Looking north from Chapel Street, the eye rests upon two parallel lines of elms extending far into the distance and forming an arch of grand proportions, decked in robes of the most delicate shades of green. On either side of the street are rows of trees of large growth, finely trimmed and each tree set out a certain distance from its neighbor. Though the street is of good width, the branches of the trees on one side of the way have long since locked arms with those of the trees on the other, completing an arch of unequalled beauty, and one upon which the admirer of nature never becomes weary of looking. The sight round about Temple Street, within the Green, too, is one of uncommon attractiveness, noble shade trees

extending in rows around every side of the enclosure, those just outside the fence, at the angles, having unusual age and size and casting
shade accordingly. Broad walks extend diagonally through and from
side to side of the grounds, and nearly every walk has an arch of over-
hanging trees. The portion of the Green left unshaded — less than
one-fourth — serves as a play and parade ground, and in summer possesses all the beauty of a well-kept lawn. The loveliness of the spot
doubtless had much to do with the choice of the place as the site of
the church edifices of three of the oldest religious organizations in
New Haven. First in order as the visitor passes along is :—

TRINITY CHURCH. — Trinity Church, on the west side of Temple
Street and just within the Green, on the Chapel Street side, is the
property of the first Episcopal parish organized in New Haven. The
edifice is built of stone of dark shades, and has a square tower of the
same material rising from the centre of the front, to a height of 100
feet. Flourishing ivies cover considerable portions of the exterior of
the walls, extending, not infrequently, over the beautiful stained glass
windows. Though erected two-thirds of a century ago (1814–15), and
though quite simple in construction, Trinity Church is yet an attractive
edifice both externally and internally. Previous to becoming settled in
the present structure, Trinity Parish, like the pioneers of all other
denominations in New Haven and elsewhere, had a somewhat interesting career. As early as 1737 the Rev. Mr. Arnold of West Haven
made a movement to establish the Episcopal Church in New Haven,
but, upon attempting to secure possession of the land on which Trinity
Church now stands, was driven away by force. Eleven years later,
Rev. Ebenezer Punderson, in 1750, on the Sunday after the Yale
Commencement, preached in the State House, and two years after
that, under his supervision the first Episcopal Church edifice was built.
It was of wood, 40 × 60 feet in size, with a steeple and chancel, and
stood on the east side of Church Street, about midway between Chapel
and Centre streets. Trinity Parish worshipped there until the comple-

tion of its present edifice. The Parish is a very wealthy and conservative one. Its present rector, the Rev. Edwin Harwood, has held the position nearly twenty-five years.

A few rods farther on, stands the Centre Church, described elsewhere, in connection with the University.

NORTH CHURCH.—About one square **north of Centre Church,** on the west side of Temple Street, and just within the **north edge of** the Green, is the North Church. The society worshipping **there was** constituted May 17, 1742, under the title of the White Haven **Society.** In 1771 a division **occurred, and the** seceding body was incorporated **under** the name of the **Fair Haven** Society. The White Haven **branch** worshipped **on the spot now known** as St. John Place; the Fair Haven branch **on the site of the present North** Church. After a separation **of a quarter of a** century **harmony again prevailed, and the branches were united. For a time the two places of worship were** occupied alternately, until in the years 1814 **and 1815 the present North** Church was built. The society has always been **Congregational.**

Crossing Elm Street, but continuing **on Temple Street, which is,** with its famous arch **of trees, half a mile in** length, several well-preserved houses of the **old style are** passed, **all more or** less worthy of **note.**

THE NOAH WEBSTER HOUSE.—The wooden portion of the **house** on the southwest corner of Temple and Grove streets, was built about the year 1825 by Noah Webster, author of the standard dictionary of the English language. **Dr.** Webster was a man who took a great interest in the ordinary affairs of life, as well as **in the** scholary ones to **which so** much of his attention **was devoted. He** therefore **planned to a great** extent his **house on Temple Street,** and it was by his orders that the space between the studding, **inside the** outer shell **of wood,** was entirely **built in with brick, in order that** the house might be warm in winter and cool in summer. Hence the walls are double,

SKULL AND BONES HALL.
(Page 32.)

SCROLL AND KEY HALL.
(Page 37.)

PSI UPSILON HALL.
(Page 35.)

DELTA KAPPA EPSILON HALL
(Page 34.)

throughout. Dr. Webster performed a portion of the work on his dictionary in this house, where he lived from about the time of his return from Amherst, until his death. Mr. Trowbridge, the present occupant, married a grand-daughter of Dr. Webster, for his first wife.

HILLHOUSE AVENUE.—Turning from Temple Street to the west, on Grove Street, and going one short block, then turning to the north, the visitor comes into full view of another beautiful thoroughfare, known as Hillhouse Avenue, in several respects the most delightful of all New Haven's many attractive public streets. First of all its great width and its magnificent elms will attract attention; then the lawns, which extend not only to the foot-paths, but several rods beyond, even to the street proper or carriage road, impressing one with the idea that he is passing along the driveway of some lawn of grand proportions to the mansion overloooking the scene from the high land at the north.

ST. MARY'S CHURCH.—The great stone edifice on the right, upon entering the avenue from Grove Street, is St. Mary's Roman Catholic Church, the largest in New Haven. It is frequently, on account of its size no doubt, erroneously called "The Cathedral." The stone of which it is constructed was obtained from quarries near the city, and is of such hue and texture as to give the structure a very solid appearance, and a perhaps somewhat cold look, which exposure to the weather will doubtless in a few years soften. St. Mary's was built ten years ago, at a cost of about $150,000. The remains of Father Murphy, who was instrumental in building the church, were buried in the little plot of ground between the main and southern entrances.

RESIDENCES.—Just north of St. Mary's is the dwelling of Mrs. William Hillhouse. The extensive brown mansion directly over the way from St. Mary's Church, on the west side of the avenue, is the residence of one of Yale's great benefactors, Mr. Joseph E. Sheffield, whose gifts to the Scientific Department have enabled it to secure the praise now everywhere so generously accorded. Mr. Sheffield's residence and the buildings of the school named for him are literally within stone's throw of one another. **Passing over the** bridge of the Northampton Railroad, the buff-colored residence **on the southwest** corner of Hillhouse Avenue and Trumbull Street is **that of Professor James D. Dana.** On the southeast corner of Hillhouse Avenue **and Trumbull** Street, is the residence of Mr. H. C. Kingsley, Treasurer **of Yale** College, while on the opposite corner resides Professor George **P.** Fisher, of the Theological Department, Yale. The remaining residences on the east side of the avenue are, in the order given, those of **President Porter, Mrs.** Collins, Mr. George H. Farnam, Mr. Henry Farnam, Professor J. M. Hoppin, Mr. **J.** M. B. Dwight and of Mrs. Pelatiah Perit. **On the** west **side, north of Trumbull** Street, are the residences of Professor Silliman, Mr. **R. A. Bigelow, the late** Mayor Skinner, Miss Davenport and **Professor Theodore S. Woolsey,** respectively.

The grand old **estate at** the head of **Hillhouse Avenue is the property** of the descendants of Hon. James Hillhouse, **to whom New** Haven is, in a great measure, indebted for the thousands of **beautiful** elms which have added so much to the fame and beauty of **the city.**

PROSPECT STREET.—Turning **to** the west, **on** Sachem's Lane, and passing along **one** block, the visitor will reach Prospect Street, ascending which, a lovely view of the western and southern portions of the city may be obtained. West **Rock is** seen in the distance, while the vast **brick structure west of and within** the shadow of the hill is **the Winchester Repeating Arms Company's** Works, where annually **are manufactured thousands of the famous Winchester rifles.** Nearly **every one of the beautiful houses on Prospect Hill has** been built **within a few years. Among the number are those of** Judge Luzon B. **Morris, Mr. D. C. Eaton,** Professor **O. C. Marsh,** Mr. W. H. Farnam, **Mr. C. H. Farnam, and Mr. E. C.** Winchester.

St. Francis Orphan Asylum and Whitney Avenue.
—Continuing on through the grove known as Sachem's Wood, Whitney Avenue may be reached by way of Highland Street, which turns off toward the east, and on which, under the brow of the hill, is the St. Francis Orphan Asylum, a Roman Catholic charitable institution which annually does a vast deal of good for poor and friendless children. The large, new brick building now used for the asylum, was completed and consecrated in 1876. It has accommodations for about two hundred children. The number at present in the asylum is about one hundred and seventy. On the first floor are parlors, sitting-rooms, dining-rooms, etc. On the second floor, school-rooms and the rooms of the Mother Superior and the Sisters of Charity. On the upper floors are the chapel, sleeping-rooms, etc. The building, which is admirably adapted to its purposes, is to a great extent the result of the untiring labors of the late Rev. Father Hart. The cost of the structure was about $75,000.

Continuing down the hill to Whitney Avenue, and proceeding northerly for perhaps half a mile, Whitneyville is reached. Here may be seen the charming little Whitney Lake; also the Whitney Rifle Factory, established by the renowned Eli Whitney, inventor of the cotton-gin. East Rock towers above the village, on the east.

In returning to the city, over Whitney Avenue, the visitor will pass several large and beautiful estates.

Orange Street, parallel with and east of Whitney Avenue, is also lined with handsome residences. Among the number is that of Governor Bigelow.

Whitney Avenue continues into Church Street on the south. Grove Hall, the large, old-fashioned house at the north end of the street, at its junction with Whitney Avenue, is a boarding school for young ladies. The residence of ex-President Woolsey of Yale is near the southwest corner of Church and Grove streets, while at number 246 Church Street resides Professor William D. Whitney. Number 226 was the home of the late Professor Lewis R. Packard.

REV. DR. LEONARD BACON'S RESIDENCE.— The large, brown dwelling-house number 247 Church Street, just north of Wall Street, for a long series of years occupied by the late Reverend Dr. Leonard Bacon, formerly stood on the ground where is now the Tontine Hotel, at the corner of Church and Court streets, and was moved to its present site, many years ago, to make room for that building. Besides the fact that this house was occupied by Dr. Bacon it possesses historic interest. During the Revolution, it was the residence of William Chandler, who turned traitor to the colony and conducted the British into the town when it was captured by them in 1779. When the troops were withdrawn Chandler and his family moved down to Nova Scotia. At one time, in the earliest days of the settlement, Ezekiel Cheevers, the first school teacher in the New Haven colony, lived on the present site of Rev. Dr. Bacon's house. Writing about Cheevers, "the last survivor of all his pupils gave it as his most distinct reminiscence of the famous grammar-school master that he wore a long white beard terminating in a point, and that when he stroked his beard to a point, it was a sign for the boys to stand clear."

CHURCH OF THE REDEEMER.—The beautiful sand-stone trimmed brick church edifice on the south-west corner of Orange and Wall streets, one block east of Church Street, is the Church of the Redeemer, Congregational. The church is Gothic-shaped, and presents an elegant appearance both outside and inside. The interior, finely furnished, contains, besides the audience room, the Sabbath School room, church parlors, etc., all excellently fitted up.

HILLHOUSE HIGH SCHOOL.—The Hillhouse High School stands diagonally opposite the Church of the Redeemer on the north-east corner of Orange and Wall streets, and is at once an honor and an ornament to the beautiful city whose property it is. The edifice is of brick, is four stories high, has handsome sandstone ornaments, and is heavily buttressed. A tower, containing a public clock, rises from the south-west corner. On the first floor are the rooms of the Board of Education and of the Superintendent and Secretary of Schools; also several recitation-rooms, janitor's room and the laboratory. On the second and third floors are study, recitation and dressing rooms, and on the fourth floor, recitation-rooms and a fine large hall in which are celebrated the graduating exercises, etc. Altogether there are eighteen rooms, with a capacity for seating a total of 400 pupils. The building was erected in 1872 at a cost, inclusive of land and furniture, of about $125,000. It is but one of about twenty-five school buildings owned or occupied by New Haven. The census of 1880 shows that there were in New Haven at that time 13,897 persons of school age. Of that number nearly 12,000 were actually registered on the school records. The total number of teachers is 232. New Haven's public schools are second to none and are equalled by very few. Visitors are perfectly welcome to visit them at any time.

CHURCH OF THE MESSIAH. — A short distance south, on the west side of Orange Street, stands the cosey Universalist Church and parsonage, recently built. This church is the only one of the Universalist denomination in the city. Established in 1852, the society worshipped for some years at the corner of Court and State streets, then, in 1865, purchased what is now the New Haven Opera House, and continued to worship there until the completion of the present edifice. The somewhat noted lady preacher, Rev. Phebe Hannaford, was pastor of this society for several years.

Continuing southerly on Orange Street, the visitor soon reaches Elm Street, on which are several fine old residences.

THE REYNOLDS HOUSE.—The Reynolds house, Number 20, Elm Street, stands on the site of the house built and occupied by John Davenport, the first minister and the leading spirit in the settlement of New Haven. The stones composing the cellar walls of the Reynolds house are the same that were used by the old dominie. Theophilus Eaton, "the Governor and true head" of the New Haven colony, lived on the opposite side of the street. His was a "grand house" furnished with "Turkey hangings," and had some fourteen fire-places.

The brown sandstone edifice on the south side of Elm Street, a short distance west of Orange Street, is St. Thomas's Episcopal Church. The parish was organized Feb. 24, 1848. Rev. Dr. E. E. Beardsley was installed as rector on the 23d of the following April, and has served continuously up to the present time — a period of a third of a century.

THE SARGENT MANSION.—The spacious brick mansion on the northwest corner of Elm and Church streets, was built by Mr. D. C. De Forest, who was for many years a merchant in Brazil. Returning to New Haven with a large property, he proceeded to erect this house, which was completed February 22,—Washington's Birthday,—1821. The christening or "house-warming" occurred on that day, and was one of the most stirring social events that New Haven had up to that time ever witnessed. Among the guests was every individual, from master-builder to apprentice boy, who had taken part in the erection of the edifice. But two members of that merry company, now venerable citizens, survive to tell the tale. Some years ago the house was purchased by Mr. Sargent, principal of the great manufacturing firm of Sargent & Co., and it was by him thoroughly rebuilt and enlarged, so that to-day it is one of the best appointed mansions in the city of New Haven, while in size very few residences anywhere exceed it.

A few rods south of Elm Street, on Church and Court streets, are several public buildings, large, costly and handsome.

CITY HALL.—The City Hall, on Church Street, north of Court Street, and facing the Green, is one of the finest municipal buildings in New England. It was built in 1861 by the city of New Haven and the town of New Haven jointly. The material used in the front of the structure is dressed sandstone, while the side-walls are of brick. A very large tower rises from the northwestern angle to a considerable height. In this tower is an illuminated public clock and two large bells; one connected with the clock and the other with the telegraphic fire alarm. On the first floor are various town offices, janitor's rooms, etc.; on the second floor, the Mayor's office, Assessors' office, the City Clerk's office, the aldermanic chamber, Road Commissioners' and other rooms; and on the third floor, the Fire Commissioners' room, Chief Engineer's office, Common Council chamber, and City Engineer's office. On the fourth floor is the battery-room of the fire telegraph, and storage rooms. The basement contains the city morgue. It will perhaps seem strange to many visitors to find the offices of a town and of a city in the same building, but the anomaly may be briefly explained by stating that the town of New Haven embraces all of the city of New Haven, together with the suburbs known as Westville and Fair Haven East. The New Haven town officers have entire control of certain branches of the public service for both New Haven City, West-ville and Fair Haven East, while the city officers have charge of all other departments in the city, their power extending to the city limits only. The various city departments are under the immediate super-vision of boards of commissioners.

COUNTY COURT BUILDING.—Immediately north of, and con-nected with, the City Hall on Church Street, is the New Haven County Court Building. The front is of dark sandstone, while polished granite pillars support the portico of the principal entrance. The first session of court held within its walls occurred Jan. 20, 1873. Since that time all sessions of the Court of Common Pleas and of the Superior Court in New Haven County have been held there. The building is admirably adapted to the purposes for which it was built. On the first floor are the offices of the Sheriff, County Commissioners, Court of Common Pleas, and vault; also the Common Pleas Court Room, with retiring rooms for the judges, the jury and the members of the bar, opening into it. On the second floor are the offices of the

State Attorney, Clerk of the Superior Court, and vault, a library and committee room 44 × 16 feet, and the Superior Court Room with retiring rooms similar to those on the first floor. The third floor is occupied by the Yale Law School, described elsewhere. The entire cost of the building, including the furniture throughout, and all extras, was about $134,000. David R. Brown, of New Haven, was the architect. The celebrated Hayden case, in which Rev. H. H. Hayden was charged with the murder of Mary Stannard, was tried in the New Haven Court-house.

THE POLICE BUILDING.—The handsome large building on the north side of Court Street, a few rods east of Church Street, and connecting at the rear with the City Hall, is the Police Department Building. It is "believed to be the most handsome and the best constructed edifice of the kind in the country." The building is a four-story brick one, having a front of Philadelphia brick, neatly ornamented with Portland sandstone and Nova Scotia stone. A Mansard roof surmounts the whole, and at the southwest corner rises a shapely and well-proportioned tower, giving to the building a pleasing outline. The edifice contains admirable conveniences for the entire police department and for the City Court and its officers. It was completed in the spring of 1874 and cost, with furnishings, about $75,000. Connected with the department to which it belongs is a force consisting of one chief, one captain, one lieutenant and eighty-one patrolmen, all under the control of a board of commissioners. The department in organization and discipline compares favorably with any in the country.

THE JEWISH SYNAGOGUE.—The Jewish Synagogue, on the north side of Court Street, between Orange and State streets, was formerly the church of the Third Congregational Society. The Jewish Congregation, Mishkan Israel, now owning the structure, was organized in 1844, and held its first meetings on Grand Street, near Artisan.

MEDICAL SCHOOL.
(Page 50.)

SLOANE LABORATORY.
(Page 31.)

The congregation is one of the largest and wealthiest of the Jewish belief in New England. Its services are, of course, held on Saturday. Quite often Christians attend, especially at Confirmation.

TONTINE PROPERTY.—The somewhat ancient but well-preserved brick structure on the southeast corner of Church and Court streets, known as the Tontine Building, is a property held under a decidedly peculiar and interesting charter, and deserves special mention. The company is of the nature of a joint stock organization, and was incorporated in 1824 by the Legislature, then sitting in New Haven. Article second of the act sets forth the peculiarities of the organization as follows: "The owner of each of said shares shall have and receive the profits or dividends on said share during the natural life of the person described opposite to his name, as nominee for such share; and upon the death of any such nominee, the share depending on the life of such nominee is to cease; and the whole profits of the said premises and of all the property of this corporation shall continually go to and be divided among such of the said owners, whose nominees shall be living at 12 o'clock at noon on the first day of March in each year, until the said nominees shall by death be reduced to seven, when the whole of said property shall vest in the names of the said seven surviving nominees, as an estate in fee simple, and this corporation shall then cease and be determined." The proposed building was completed in 1827. Of the original number of nominees, 243, there are at present living 125. They are of all grades of society, and are scattered all over the globe, making it a matter of much difficulty for the secretary to keep the mortuary record. It is doubtful if any of the original stockholders are living, and the stock is held by those who acquired possession through purchase or inheritance.

THIRD CHURCH.—The house of worship on Church Street, a few rods north of Chapel Street, belongs to the Third Congregational Society, instituted, September 6, 1826. The building is of brownstone, and was erected in 1856. **Formerly it was surmounted by a graceful,** but unfortuately very weak, steeple. **The constant·fear that it would** be blown down in a gale caused the society to have the steeple removed **in 1877.**

This completes the trip **through the northern section of the city.**

SOUTHERN NEW HAVEN.

GENERAL DESCRIPTION.—The southern portion of New Haven is in some respects the most interesting section of the "City of Elms." For years after the settlement of the town a majority of the inhabitants lived in the vicinity of what are now known as George, Meadow, and West Water streets; and the burden of commerce was carried on there. Quite a number of the residences of "ye olden time" are yet standing. The most convenient route to this section is through Church Street, on which, south of Chapel Street, the point of starting, are many business houses, blocks, and the post-office.

THE POST-OFFICE AND CUSTOM HOUSE.—On the west side of Church Street, midway between Crown and Centre streets, is the post-office and custom house—a large sandstone structure built by the government in 1860 for the purposes to which it is now devoted. The first floor is used exclusively by the post-office department. Mr. N. D. Sperry, the postmaster, has held the position for more than twenty consecutive years. The second floor of the building is the custom house, and is partitioned off into offices for the collector of customs, the inspector, gaugers, etc., while on the third floor is the United States Court room, with judges' rooms attached. It is said that a New Haven postmaster was the first in the United States to adopt the use of postage stamps, issuing them on his own account to accommodate citizens who desired to mail letters at times when the post-office was not open to receive cash for postage.

HOADLEY BUILDING.—The handsome great marble block on the north-east corner of Church and Crown streets, known as the Hoadley Building, is worthy of mention on its own account, and also, because the ground it occupies is the spot on which stood the hotel where La Fayette was entertained on his visit to New Haven more than half a century ago. For many years this hotel was the leading public house in New Haven, and was the place where all public dinners in celebration of national and other great events were given. It was in that hotel that the great jubilee dinner in honor of the announcement of peace in the War of 1812 occurred. This dinner was the most elaborate that, up to that time, had ever been given in New Haven. President Monroe visited New Haven during his administration (1817–1825) and dined at this hotel. One Butler was the proprietor. "The President said it was the best dinner he ever sat down to, and Butler, who had prepared the dinner, and who was a rough-speaking man, replied with one of his great words, 'Gracious! I am now ready to die!' for Butler was indeed famed for his dinners, and this compliment from the President of the United States completely satisfied his ambition."

BENEDICT ARNOLD'S BRIDAL HOME.—The large, unpainted house on the north side of George Street, just west of Church Street and numbered 87, is the residence in which Benedict Arnold passed the first few years of his married life. His father-in-law, Mr. Moses Mansfield, who lived where the Grand Opera House or Music Hall now stands, owned the house on George Street, and gave to young Arnold and his bride the use of the house as a sort of wedding present. Arnold's place of business, a druggist's store, stood but a few feet east of the house, at the corner of Church and George Streets, on the site of the large brick structure known as Wood's Block.

THE OLDEST HOUSE IN NEW HAVEN.—The large, antique wooden building on Meadow Street, numbered 177, and standing but a few rods south of Church Street, is the oldest house in New Haven. It was built in 1642, four years after the settlement of the town, and was one of the houses known in early colonial history as a blue house, from the fact that at that time every house was painted either red or blue. The color was indicated on the old maps by the initial letters R or B, according as the house was one hue or the other. For those days the Meadow Street house must have been a mansion with few equals in cost or excellence in America. It is larger than many of the dwellings of to-day, and is still a very comfortable residence. The house was built by Mr. Joseph Trowbridge, one of the pioneers.

The little, narrow, crooked street, now called Prout Street, extending from Meadow to State Street, has for over two hundred years been known as " Peggy's Elbow," it being exactly in the shape of a bended arm.

THE HUNT HOUSE AND THE JEWS' RETREAT.—The Hunt House, on Meadow Street near Water Street, is probably, with the exception of the Trowbridge House in Meadow Street, the oldest dwelling in New Haven. The front east room on the first floor, was the place where Benedict Arnold taught the young men of New Haven the sword exercise just before the War of the Revolution. Until within a few years there stood opposite this house a building containing six distinct, large, roomy tenements. It was known as the "long house." At the time of its erection, it was said that it was to accommodate the Jews, who were at that time (1800) being driven to this country by harsh laws in Europe.

NEAR THE DEPOTS.—On the northeast corner of Water and Meadow streets is the Totten house, built years before the Revolution. At that period there lived in the house Captain Rice, a sturdy loyalist. With him, at the time of the invasion of New Haven by the British, dined several of the King's officers, and through the interces-

sion of Captain Rice the enemy spared many of the fine houses in the
neighborhood from pillage and burning.   In ancient times, some years
after the colony of New Haven **was founded,** the land directly opposite this house, where the Derby passenger station now is, was the
ship-yard of William Greenough, **the most** extensive shipbuilder who
ever occupied the yard.

The long, brick, Mansard-roof edifice, east of this point **on Union**
Avenue, near the southern end of Meadow Street, is the depot **of the**
New York, New Haven & Hartford Railroad. The restaurant in **the**
waiting-room of this depot is kept by Mr. S. H. Moseley, of the New
Haven House, **and is one** of the best in the country.

The brick building **on the** southwest corner of Columbus and
Christopher Streets, **was one of the first** dwellings built of brick in
the colony, having been erected about 1773. Its owner and occupant,
Thomas Trowbridge, was an officer in the Revolutionary Army, and
died a prisoner on board the Jersey prison-ship in New York Harbor,
in 1782.

HOUSES AND CHURCHES. — The large modern house, 217 Water
Street, **was** erected **over** a century since, and for many years was the
residence of Captain Gad Peck, a famous navigator and shipowner in
his day. **In** the War of 1812, while in the West India seas in command of the " Mohawk " (a beautiful New Haven-built ship) he was
captured by a French privateer; but a few nights afterwards he and
his crew re-took the ship and brought her home to New Haven.

West Haven, a beautiful seaside **suburb of** New Haven, may be
reached from this point *via* Portsea Street, Howard and Kimberly
Avenues.

The Church of the Sacred **Heart** (Roman Catholic) is the plain,
massive sandstone structure at the southwest corner **of** Columbus
and Liberty Streets. It was formerly the South Reformed Church.
The tower contains a bell of very superior tone.

The attractive stone church on the southwest corner of Howard

Avenue and Columbus Street, is the **Howard Avenue** Congregational **Church.**

St. Bernard Cemetery. — St. Bernard Cemetery, near the junction of Davenport and Columbus Avenues, is the principal **Roman** Catholic burying-ground in the city. It embraces twenty-seven acres of land. Efforts are now in progress by which the **appearance of** the grounds will be much improved. **St. Bernard's was consecrated Sep-** tember 2, 1851, by Rt. Rev. Bernard O'Reilly.

Evergreen Cemetery. — Evergreen Cemetery, at the western **extremity of Sylvan** Avenue, is a well-laid-out burying-ground border- **ing on West River.** Within its limits are the two largest monuments **in the city, —** the Soldiers' Memorial and the Firemen's. The Soldiers' **monument** stands on Evergreen Avenue, but a short distance from the entrance. It is a shaft of granite surmounted by a granite figure of a soldier standing at parade rest. On the monument are inscribed the names of the fallen heroes, one hundred and **twenty of** whom **were** interred in the **lot on which the monument stands. The monument** was erected by the **State of Connecticut.** The **Firemen's monument,** on Highland Avenue, overlooking **West** River, **is** of granite, sur- mounted by a bronze statue of a fireman in uniform. Bronze tablets near the **base** of the monument bear, in relief, representations em- blematic **of the life of a fireman.** The monument was erected by the Firemen's Benevolent Association, of New Haven. There are, in the cemetery, many beautiful private monuments, including those belong- ing to Governor English, H. M. Welch, E. A. Mitchell and Massena **Clark, on Prospect** Avenue; Governor Bigelow, on Highland Avenue; **and C. D.** Murray, on Western Avenue.

The New Haven Hospital. — The New Haven Hospital **on** Cedar Street, Congress, Davenport and Howard Avenues, occupies, with land and buildings, an entire square. In the summer of 1833, the hospital, then consisting of a substantial stone building, was opened for patients. One after another of the various structures now on the grounds has been erected as necessity required and funds permitted. The handsome, great, new brick building, at once attracting the gaze of the visitor, was built in 1872, at a cost, with furnishings, of nearly $100,000. The length of the building is 264 feet, and it has a capacity for 120 patients. There is a central portion devoted to attendants' rooms, dining and store-rooms, with two wings extending from it in opposite directions, in which are the wards for the patients on three floors. Ample provision has been made for escape in case of fire. The old portion of the hospital, west of and connecting with the new building, is used for offices, store-rooms, rooms for attaches, etc. The New Haven Hospital has done and is doing now an immense amount of good for suffering humanity, and is a prominent one of the many noble institutions of which the "City of Elms" is possessed. Although the rules provide that "no physician or surgeon shall receive any compensation for his services," the hospital commands the skill of a number of the very foremost physicians in the city and State.

ST. JOHN'S CATHOLIC CHURCH.—St. John's Roman Catholic Church, directly over the way from the hospital grounds towards the north, at the junction of Davenport Avenue and York Street, stands upon the site of the first Catholic church erected in New Haven. As far back as 1779, when Baron de la Chambeau's army was passing through the town, a chaplain of the Baron said mass in camp near the present St. Bernard cemetery in the southwestern part of the city; and this is thought to have been the first Roman Catholic service held in New Haven. A paper published Jan. 28, 1796, announced that "a Roman Catholic priest is in New Haven, where he will reside some time." The first recorded case, however, of mass celebrated in New Haven by a secular clergyman, did not occur until 1826, when Dr. Powers, of New York, held a service at the head of Long Wharf.

Eight years later, 1834, the first Catholic church was built, on the site of the present St. John's Church, and was burned in 1848. The present edifice was erected in 1858. For years St. John's parish was presided over by Rev. Hugh Carmody, one of the most learned and esteemed Roman Catholic clergymen in the diocese.

Passing northerly from this point, two blocks, on Broad Street, the visitor will find himself in the vicinity of the Home for Aged Women of Trinity Parish and of the :—

CHURCHES ON GEORGE STREET.—The Home for Aged Women of Trinity Parish, situated on the north side of George Street, between College and High streets, was erected in 1869 by the munificence of Mr. Joseph E. Sheffield. The Home consists of three substantial, ornamental buildings, two of which are surmounted by graceful turrets.

The church at the southeast corner of George and Broad streets belongs to the German Baptist society, while that at 133 and 135 George Street is the property of the German Methodist society. A short distance south, at 125 George Street, standing back from the highway, is the German Catholic Church.

The Grand Opera House, formerly Music Hall, on the south side of Crown Street, a few rods west of Church Street, seats about twenty-five hundred persons.

From Music Hall the visitor may reach the point of starting *via* Crown and Church streets.

Eastern New Haven.

General Description.—Eastern New Haven is eminently the business **and manufacturing** portion of the city. Many of the **streets are completely lined with** stores and warehouses, while others **are filled with** manufactories. **Portions of** the district, however, are occupied **with dwellings, many of** which **are** as **fine as any in the city.** New Haven's peculiarity of building residences and **factories in the** same locality is strikingly exemplified in this part of the city.

Chapel Street to State Street.—Chapel **Street, the principal** business thoroughfare of the city, is completely **taken up, between** Church and Union streets, with stores, banks, offices, etc. Many of the blocks are large, and are of an attractive style of archi**tecture.** The stores are devoted almost wholly to retail trade. Just **north** of Chapel Street, on Orange Street, is Odd Fellows' Hall, occupying the upper story of the Palladium Building—the large sandstone **block on** the east side of the street. The building takes its title from **the** Palladium newspaper, one **of the five** bright, enterprising and **thoroughly newsy dailies published in** New Haven: the " Morning **Journal and** Gourier " (Rep.**),** the " Morning Palladium " (Rep.), the **" Morning News "** (Ind.), **the "** Evening Register " (Dem.**),** and the **" Evening Union "** (Ind.**).**

Chapel Street is crossed, **one block east of Orange** Street, by State Street, **on which** are situated many wholesale establishments.

OLDEST BRICK HOUSE IN NEW HAVEN.—On the east side of State Street, just north of Elm Street, stands the oldest brick house in New Haven. It is one story high, with "gambrel" roof, and was built by a Mr. Pinto, a native of Trinidad, West Indies, who carried on business in New Haven about the time of the Revolutionary War. It is probable that the house was built in 1770 or thereabouts. At pres-. ent it is used as a store. What may be called the twin of this house, built perhaps a little later, stands on George Street near Broad Street.

About one mile and a half northeast of this point is East Rock, reached *via* State Street. St. John's Episcopal Church, at the northwest corner of State and Eld streets, and the Skinner School Building, as well as several large factories, are passed on the way. The German quarter of the city lies a short distance west of State Street and north of Edwards Street.

EAST ROCK.—East Rock, the perpendicular eminence at the northeast of the city, is two miles from the City Hall, and about the same distance from its fellow, West Rock. About 354 feet high, and affording an excellent view of New Haven and its suburbs, the summit of East Rock is much more accessible than that of West Rock, a carriage road leading to the top, from the east side, while a stairway affords a way of ascending the front itself of the great precipice. The State Street Line horse cars pass under the very shadow of the east end of the Rock. To the west of East Rock are seen Mill Rock, Pine Rock and West Rock, in the order mentioned. Whitneyville and Lake Whitney lie at the foot of East Rock on the north, while the city proper, the harbor, and West Haven are seen on the south and west. To the southeast and east are Fair Haven and Fair Haven East, both belonging to New Haven, the stream flowing at the foot of East Rock separating Fair Haven from the city proper, or old New Haven, and the river still further to the east separating Fair Haven from Fair Haven East—a district recently annexed to the town and extending to the light-house on Long Island Sound, four miles distant. The annexation was made in order that New Haven might secure better control of its harbor. A recently demolished house on the top of East Rock was owned and occupied by the owner of the Rock, who lived there many years, and who secured not a little money in the summer months by charging a small fee (ten cents) to all who visited the summit of the eminence, *via* the stairs above mentioned. In the early part of the present century, there lived on the Rock a hermit, Elias Turner. He was very peculiar, rarely speaking to any one, and seeming content with the most scanty clothing and the meanest shelter. Dame Rumor attributed his wretched condition to " the pangs of despised love.' One morn he was " missed on the 'customed hill," and on the second of November, 1823, was found in his hovel cold in death. East Rock is embraced in the plan for a large and ornamental park of 371 acres in the vicinity of the northeastern section of the city.

THE MANUFACTURING DISTRICT. — Proceeding *via* State to Hamilton Street, thence to St. John Street, the visitor is in the midst of an immense manufacturing district. On Hamilton, St. John and Wallace streets is the vast factory of the New Haven Clock Company, while but one block distant, on Green, Wallace and East streets are the works of the L. Candee Rubber Company, manufacturers of rubber boots and shoes. The great lock and key factory of Mallory & Wheeler is within a stone's throw, at the foot of Green Street. Every one of these concerns constantly employs several hundred persons. In the immediate neighborhood are vast foundries, carriage manufactories, etc., etc., in large numbers.

FAIR HAVEN AND FAIR HAVEN EAST. — A beautiful drive may be taken from this point through Grand Street to Fair Haven, passing St. Patrick's Catholic Church, a substantial brick edifice at the corner of Grand and Wallace streets *en route*. Fair Haven, comprising two wards of the city, is a well-laid-out and handsome suburb whose chief industry has been and is the cultivation of oysters, ιarge beds of an excellent quality of which have existed there for centuries. There are also several large manufactories, comprising planing mills, rolling mills, and the iron works of Governor Bigelow. There are several costly churches in the district, including the First Congregational Church, Grand Street; Grace Episcopal Church, Blatchley Avenue; St. Francis Roman Catholic Church, just north of Grand Street, and the Pearl Street Methodist Church, Pearl Street.

Crossing the Grand Street bridge into Fair Haven East, the house of worship on the right, at the corner of Grand and Quinnipiac streets, is the church of which John S. C. Abbott the historian was the pastor. From the heights just east of the church, a lovely view of the city is obtained.

Four miles down the shore is the Old Light-house. The drive there is a very pleasant one in summer, affording a fine prospect of the harbor and of several points of great historic interest.

FORTS HALE AND WOOSTER. — Fort Wooster, on the heights east of the road, and about a mile below the city, is an earthwork, hastily thrown up during the War of 1812. The embankments are still visible. One mile south of Fort Wooster, on a rock extending into the harbor, is Fort Hale, originally improvised as a point of defence in the Revolutionary War. Here it was that nineteen Americans with three field pieces, on the afternoon of July 5, 1779, bade defiance to fifteen hundred British troops, and continued to fight until overborne by sheer force of numbers. In 1809, a brick fort and barracks were built on the spot, and in the War of 1812, the place was garrisoned by about sixty men. During the American Civil War the government rebuilt the fort, armed and garrisoned it, and everything was made ready to resist attack. Fort Hale was named in honor of Captain Nathan Hale, the hero of the Revolution.

THE MORRIS HOUSE AND THE LIGHT-HOUSE. — The Morris house, about a mile south of Fort Hale, is one of the most interesting buildings within the limits of New Haven. It was built in 1672, of split granite taken from land in the vicinity. The mortar in which the stones were laid was made of oyster shells found on the beach, and the timber was cut on the estate. In 1779, at the time of the invasion by the British, the house was burned. The walls remained, however, and the interior was rebuilt. Before the fire there were sixteen large rooms in the structure. Ever since it was built the house has been owned by the Morris family. The present proprietor, J. H. Morris, Esq., represents the eighth successive generation that has lived there. The well on the place was dug when the house was built, and is still the source of supply of drinking water for the family.

The Old Light-house, a short distance south of the Morris place, is at the mouth of New Haven harbor, and was built many years ago. Within a few years, the new light-house on a ledge a few hundred yards southwest of the old one, has superseded the latter in usefulness.

Returning over the shore road and crossing the long, covered structure known as Tomlinson's bridge, the city proper is again reached. Within a hundred feet of the city end of the bridge are the docks of the New Haven Steamboat Company, while a moment's ride west of the docks, are :—

THE PAVILION AND SARGENT'S FACTORY.—The extensive but somewhat dilapidated building on the northeast corner of Water and Wallace streets, just east of the great factory of Sargent & Co., was erected about 1810, and was a famous hostelry in its day. Under its roof tarried many of the most distinguished men of the country. At that time there were no buildings in front of the Pavilion, as the house was called, and an unobstructed view was had of the harbor and of Long Island Sound. Many West India families, and many prominent families from the South made the Pavilion their summer residence. Of late years the building has been used as a tenement or boarding-house, and shows signs of neglect, though its peculiar architecture and unusual size still at once attract the eye of the passer-by.

Sargent & Co.'s factory, occupying a vast territory on East Street, in the vicinity of Wallace and Hamilton streets, is the largest concern in the world where small iron work of almost every conceivable description is carried on. Nine thousand different styles of articles,—from a toy spade to the finest of locks,—are made there, requiring the constant labor of twelve hundred persons.

Passing northerly through Wallace Street into Chapel Street, several extensive carriage and other factories are passed. A short distance west of this point is :—

WOOSTER SQUARE. — It is a beautiful park, shaded by numerous elms, and is surrounded by substantial dwellings, churches, schools, etc. The "Collegiate and Commercial Institute" of General William H. Russell, fronts on Wooster Place, opposite Wooster Square. Established nearly half a century ago, it has prepared hundreds of students for entrance to the great University in New Haven, and as many more to enter upon the duties of practical life.

CHURCHES. — Standing on the corner of Wooster Place and Green Street is the First Baptist Church, better known as the Wooster Place Church. The large wooden dome gives the structure an entirely different appearance from any other church edifice in New Haven. The organization of the society worshipping there was effected October 30, 1816, and is the oldest parish of the Baptist denomination in the city. The first meetings were held at Amos Doolittle's lodge-room on the west side of College Street, a short distance north of Elm Street.

The church diagonally opposite the northeast angle of Wooster Square, on Green Street, belongs to the Davenport Congregational Society.

On the southeast corner of Chapel and Olive streets is the twin-turreted stone church of St. Paul's Episcopal Parish.

NEW HAVEN OPERA HOUSE. — The dark-brown Grecian building a short distance west of St. Paul's Church, on the south side of Chapel Street, is the New Haven Opera House, a well-arranged and very cosey little theatre with a large and convenient stage, a single balcony and four boxes. It seats about one thousand persons. The building was formerly the First Baptist Church, then became the Universalist Church, and in 1877 was converted to its present use.

MASONIC TEMPLE. — The Masonic Temple, situated on the southeast corner of Chapel and Union streets, was built during the year 1872. The corner-stone was laid by the Grand Lodge of the State of Connecticut, December 6, 1871. The building was completed in October, 1872, and the rooms occupied by the Masonic Fraternity were dedicated by the Grand Lodge, October 16, 1872. The first floor of the building is used for stores; the second floor, for offices; and the third floor, by the Blues Light Guard, and the Governor's Foot Guard, for company and drill rooms. The Masonic fraternity occupy the remaining portion of the building, comprising sixteen rooms. Entering from the south stairs, one is ushered into the tyler's room, adjoining which are two parlors, about twelve feet square each. The lodge-room proper is one of the largest in the country, being 62 feet long by 41 feet wide, with a height of 22 feet. The banquet hall is 18 feet wide by 50 feet long and 22 feet high. The Chapter, Council and Commandery room is 40 by 22 feet, with a height of 18 feet. The armory for the Templars' regalias is fitted up with ninety-two cases, two regalias to a case. Dimensions of armory, 30 by 22 feet, and 12 feet in height. There are, also, on this floor, reception rooms, etc. On the floor above are the kitchen and modern conveniences. The building is in dimensions 70 feet on Chapel Street by 126 feet on Union Street, and four stories high. It cost about $100,000. The fitting up of the Masonic rooms cost about $11,000. Visitors can obtain admission upon application to the janitor, Mr. George Smith, Room 10, Masonic Building.

YALE LAW SCHOOL.
(Page 48.)

CITY HALL.
(Page 96.)

THIRD SENIOR SOCIETY HALL.

THE CITY MARKET.—Just below, or rather facing the railroad bridge, on the south side of Chapel Street, and at the corner of Union Street, is the Old Depot, or City Market. It occupies the site of the "Old City Market." For years there was a law prohibiting the sale of meat elsewhere than in the old market; and many of the citizens of New Haven distinctly remember the ill-feeling generated by this restriction. The present structure was built for a depot, in the basement of which all passenger trains on the principal lines entering the city formerly left and received passengers. The waiting and baggage rooms on the first floor are now utilized as a city market. The great square tower on the northeast corner of the structure is about 100 feet high, and contains an illuminated clock.

THE SECOND REGIMENT.—Opposite Masonic Temple, in the Collins Building, 195 Chapel Street, is the beautiful armory of the New Haven Grays. The armory proper, located on the third floor, is reached through the elegant parlors of the organization, on the second floor. The Grays constitute company F of the famous Second Connecticut Regiment, which is, perhaps, the best drilled militia organization in America. Constituted in 1739, the regiment has ever sustained a high reputation, both at home and abroad. The "Army and Navy Journal," the recognized military authority in this country, thus spoke of the organization after its visit to the Empire State in 1872: "The visit of the Second Regiment to New York, its magnificent appearance and drill, leads us to ask why the State of New York, which boasts the superiority over every other State in the Union, does not maintain it by comparison. The Second Connecticut demonstrated plainly to unbiased minds that we have but one regiment which equals it—none which excels."

THE SPOT WHERE THE PILGRIM LIVED.—The brick block on the northwest corner of Union and Fair streets, a few rods south of the old depot, occupies the site of the Isaac Allerton residence. A granite tablet placed in the Fair Street side of the block by Mr. Thomas R. Trowbridge, Jr., bears the following inscription, which explains a great deal in a very few words :—

" ISAAC ALLERTON, A PILGRIM OF THE MAYFLOWER, AND THE FATHER OF NEW ENGLAND COMMERCE, LIVED ON THIS GROUND FROM 1646 TILL 1659."

Allerton was the only Plymouth Pilgrim who ever went to New Haven. It was supposed that none of his descendants were living, but the announcement that a tablet had been erected to his memory developed the fact that there were a number of parties who could clearly trace kinship.

BENEDICT ARNOLD'S HOUSE.—A step or two east of Union Street, on Water Street, stands the residence built and for some years occupied by Benedict Arnold, the traitor. Arnold was already comfortably situated in a house on George Street, when, in 1771, he determined to build a house of his own, on Water Street. It was completed for occupancy in the summer of 1772, and there Arnold resided until the outbreak of the Revolution. His store for a time was just west of the house. While doing business there, Arnold, who was of a very speculative, restless disposition, overbearing and haughty, combined with his apothecary trade a department in West India goods. One day, a man rushing into Arnold's house, informed him that a certain party had made known to the government the secret that Arnold was smuggling this class of goods. Arnold seized a whip, searched for and found the tell-tale, and gave him a thorough cowhiding. When news of the Battle of Lexington reached New Haven Arnold was at dinner, at his house. He at once put on his accoutrements, called the Governor's Guard—of which he was commander—to arms, and marched at their head to Boston. Before leaving town, he demanded ammunition of the selectmen, which they refused, whereupon he gave them the choice of surrendering the keys to the magazine or of having it torn open. The keys were at once forthcoming, and, securing the ammunition, Arnold and his company continued their march to Boston. Arnold returned to New Haven May 8th, 1778, visited his house on Water Street, and soon after left New Haven forever. In 1781, Arnold having previously become a traitor, the property was attached by Hannah Arnold, who recovered a considerable sum, and in 1782 the house was adjudged forfeited to the State, "Benedict Arnold now having joined the enemies of the United States." It was sold, the proceeds going to the State. Some years afterward the house was the property of the great lexicographer, Noah Webster, who for a time resided there. It now belongs to the heirs of James Hunt, viz., Mrs. D. Goffe Phipps, Mrs. Evelina Jones and the heirs of Harriet D. Henriques. Many yet living can recollect the house when its spacious grounds and beautiful orchard were the admiration of every one; and the old structure of the present day will remind the passer-by of the tastes of the original proprietor and ye olden time.

THE RUTHERFORD **WAREHOUSE.**—Situated on State Street, next east of Number 107, near Water Street, is the structure built and used for many years as a warehouse by Henry Rutherford, a West India merchant who did business in New Haven from 1680 to 1700. The warehouse was built as early as 1682, and perhaps earlier. It is a low one story and a half wooden building, painted red, and contrasts wonderfully with the great wholesale warehouses of the New Haven of to-day. Formerly a creek flowed by the rear of the warehouse, so that goods were loaded with great convenience and dispatch, for those times. At present the building is occupied by a shoemaker, who plies his trade within its ancient walls. After standing for two hundred years, unharmed by fire or flood, the warehouse will soon give way to the march of improvement, as the company owning the land proposes to build a large structure on its site. However, the building will not be destroyed, but will be removed to another location and there preserved as a relic of the past.

From here the point of starting on the tour of Eastern New Haven may be reached *via* Crown, Orange and Chapel, or **Crown, Orange, Centre and Church** streets.

WESTERN NEW HAVEN.

GENERAL DESCRIPTION.—Western New Haven abounds in residences and in beautiful streets. Here and there a factory appears, and occasionally a store, but the section is taken up principally by homes. The greater part of this portion of the city is comparatively newly built, and is, generally speaking, very attractive to the eye. Chapel Street, at its intersection with Church Street, may, as in trips to the other portions of the city, be taken as a point of departure.

BUILDINGS.—The great stone structure on the south side of Chapel Street, midway between Church and Temple streets, is the Insurance Building. It is six stories high, is built of granite, contains stores and offices of various kinds, and is the headquarters of several societies and clubs, notably the Yale freshman society, Gamma Nu. On the top floor, room 46, is the United States signal station.

On the west side of Temple Street, one block south of Chapel Street, is the brownstone chapel of Trinity Episcopal Society, with rector's residence attached.

The building on the south side of Chapel Street, on the corner of Temple Street, opposite Trinity Church, was the residence of the late Admiral Foote.

The sandstone-trimmed brick chapel of the Centre Congregational Society stands a short distance back from Chapel Street, opposite the Green, while the tall drab-colored building a few rods further west is the Quinnipiac Club House.

A short distance south of Chapel Street, on College Street, stands the College Street Congregational Church, built in 1848.

VIEW OF THE GREEN. — From the corner of Chapel and College streets the visitor secures an excellent view of New Haven's pride, the Green. Other public parks may be larger, but the average citizen of New Haven always feels that the plot of ground bounded by Court, Chapel, College and Elm streets is a little superior in point of beauty to all others. The work of beautifying the Green began very long ago, and each successive generation has endeavored to add something to heighten the effect. As the visitor may see, there is a wealth of carefully trimmed elms, while the grass in summer time is always kept at just the proper height for the best appearance. Concreted paths extend in every direction. While great care is taken to keep the Green a thing of beauty, it is by no means made wholly exclusive to useful or pleasurable objects. Its convenience of access makes it at times a valuable drill and parade ground for the police and the military, while the booming of cannon within its limits is quite sure to accompany every great celebration. Formerly the Yale students resorted to the upper portion of the Green in out-door sports, but this practice the authorities were some years since obliged to forbid, owing to the impossibility under the circumstances of keeping the Green in good trim.

PROFESSOR THACHER'S RESIDENCE. — The house in which the venerable Professor Thomas C. Thacher now lives, at No. 155 Crown Street, was built for Jeremiah Day, then Professor of Mathematics and Astronomy in Yale College, by Asahel Tuttle, under a contract made, apparently, on the 31st day of August, 1815. Tuttle was owner of the land on which the house was to be built, and contracted to build the house on the land, which, after the building was completed, was to be conveyed by deed to Professor Day. The house was nearly ready for occupation, when, on the 11th day of January, 1817, the death of Timothy Dwight, President of the College, occurred, and

YALE BOAT HOUSE.
(Page 66.)

THE OBSERVATORY.
(Page 62.)

before Professor Day could move into his house, he was appointed Dr. Dwight's successor as President of the College. Having been appointed President, he asked permission of the corporation to occupy the house which he had just built. This was refused on the ground that his house was too remote from the College. The house was consequently occupied during the next twenty-nine years by others; namely, Professor Eleazar T. Fitch, Bishop Thomas C. Brownell, General Hezekiah Howe, and, from 1830 to 1846, by Professor Josiah W. Gibbs. On the 21st of October, 1846,—the day on which he inducted his successor, President Woolsey, into office,—President Day began to live in the house which he had built for himself thirty years before, and he continued to occupy it until his death, which occurred on the 22d of August, 1867. Since that date the house has been occupied, as it now is, by Professor Thacher.

COLLEGE STORES, OPERA HOUSE, ETC.—The large brick block on Chapel Street, opposite the college fence, and extending west from College Street, is taken up on the first floor by stores devoted to student interests, while the floors above are finished off into studies and sleeping apartments, rented mostly to students.

Carll's Opera House, in the rear of Chapel Street, opposite South College, is one of the three largest theatres in America, seating upwards of twenty-seven hundred persons. It has a very roomy stage, capable of accommodating the most extensive scenery, and so arranged that the heaviest machines or vehicles ever used in a stage performance may be placed on the boards with the greatest ease. The dressing-rooms attached are the largest, most convenient and best planned of any in America.

THE ROGER SHERMAN HOUSE.—The residence built and occupied by that distinguished patriot, statesman and scholar, Roger Sherman, is yet standing at Number 480 Chapel Street, opposite the college campus, and retains essentially its original appearance, the descendants of its illustrious owner having preserved it very carefully and well. The house was completed in 1770, in which year Mr. Sherman moved into it. Within its walls, preceding the Revolution, were held many discussions as to the best manner of meeting the impending difficulties with the mother country; and here, doubtless, were considered the outlines of various articles, the substance of which at length appeared in the United States Constitution, of which Roger Sherman was one of the framers. In this house, too, General Washington was entertained while on his way to take command of the American Army around Boston, and General La Fayette was a guest there, years later. In 1779, at the British invasion, Roger Sherman's house was among the first to be entered and ransacked by the redcoats, who appropriated every portable article of value in the building. Ever since the death of its original owner, the house has been occupied by his descendants.

WEST CHAPEL STREET.— Calvary Baptist Church, the tasteful brick structure on the southeast corner of Chapel and York streets, was for some years presided over by the Rev. H. M. Gallaher, now of Brooklyn, N. Y.

West Chapel Street is lined with fine residences, as are also many of the intesecting streets, including, particularly, Howe and Dwight streets.

The light gray edifice on the northwest corner of Chapel and Dwight streets is the Dwight Place Congregational Church, built in 1871. The material of which the church is composed is an artificial stone, made specially for the purpose by a process similar to that used in making concrete, though each piece was given its shape in a mould. While Moody and Sankey were engaged in revival work in New Haven in the spring of 1878, the Dwight Place Church was the one where the enquiry meetings, following the tabernacle meetings, were held.

A succession of handsome residences, including the very extensive and costly one of the late Burton Mallory, at the corner of Orchard Street, fill up the remaining half mile on Chapel Street to the West-

River. Cyrus Northrop, professor of Rhetoric and English Literature in Yale College, resided at Number 607, near Day Street.

WESTVILLE.—Crossing the bridge and **driving a** half mile to Forest Street, thence passing northerly a few minutes' ride on the latter street, Edgewood, the beautiful home **of** the distinguished author Donald G. Mitchell—"Ik Marvel"—is reached. The residence and the grounds about it are very tasteful and **very attractive.**

Continuing through **Forest Street to** Fountain, thence **to Main** Street, **the visitor reaches** Westville, **where is met, face to** face, the highest of :—

THE GREAT ROCKS ENCLOSING NEW HAVEN.—" West **Rock, Pine** Rock, Mill Rock and East **Rock stand like a broken line of ramparts along the northern confines of the** city plain, within **two miles of the College, attractive for their scenery** and forest walks, for the landscapes **to be enjoyed from their tops and for the geological** instruction they **offer. . . . . Thus these trap rocks and ridges** add greatly to the number and variety of the walks and drives about the **city. . . . .** Why the north-and-south **line of fissures in which West** Rock ridge originated **should have terminated to the** south **(at West-** ville) so abruptly, and why, at **its termination, an** east-and-west series of fractures and eruptions should have been produced across the plain from West **Rock to East Rock, giving origin to Pine Rock and Mill** Rock, are **questions** yet without answer."—*From an* **article by Pro-** *fessor James D. Dana in the Yale Book.*

WEST ROCK —West Rock, an almost perpendicular mass **of** stone rising to the height **of 405 feet, acting the** part of a grim sentinel **at the** northwest approach **to the city which it overlooks,** affords a **grand** point whence **to view New Haven and the country round about it.** Westville nestles beneath **the very shadow of** the Rock, while the city proper, **the harbor, portions of** West Haven, East Haven and Long

Island Sound, and all of **Fair Haven,** stretch forth like a huge panorama. As the Rock is nearly three miles from the centre of the city, it will be well to take a westward-bound car on the Fair Haven and Westville horse railroad to reach the vicinity. A foot-path, quite steep, but by no means difficult, offers opportunity of ascent from the east end of the Rock. The view to be obtained in a clear day will amply repay a visit to the summit. It will be well to remember, while examining the Rock, that the statement made in various publications to the effect that West Rock is the termination of the Green Mountains " is as absurd as to say that two parallel lines fifty miles apart end in a common point; in fact, more absurd than this, since the Green Mountains were made some millions of years before the trap ridges of the Connecticut Valley."

JUDGES' CAVE.—A foot-path extending in a northwesterly direction from the summit of West Rock, leads, after a walk of some minutes, to the famous Judges' Cave, a spot visited by hundreds of students and others every year. The cave consists of great fragments of a bowlder, forming a shelter under which half a dozen men or more might hide themselves. Tradition has it that Whalley and Goffe, two of the regicide judges of Charles I., took refuge in this cave to escape detection by the king's officers, who were making diligent search for them in the town. Hence the name, "Judges' Cave." The rocks of the Judges' Cave are fragments of one of the bowlders of immense size which fell from the great glacier that passed down over a large portion of North America in the glacial period. The bowlder "must have weighed, when entire, one thousand tons." It "no doubt came from some point on the high trap ridge between the Meriden Hanging Hills and Mount Tom, in Massachusetts; and must have travelled at least fifteen miles, and perhaps seventy-five."

THE BRITISH INVASION.—Returning to the city *via* Whalley Avenue, the visitor may see on the high land just east of the Westville bridge the spot where a handful of Americans under Captain Phineas Bradley fought fifteen hundred British troops, at noon on Monday the 5th of July, 1779, and attempted to prevent their entrance to the town. At sunrise on that day the King's troops, under Brigadier-General Garth, started on their march from West Haven, where they had landed a few hours before, for the purpose of invading New Haven. The two companies at first sent out were driven back by the Americans, whereupon the entire body of English troops received orders to march on the town. West Bridge—near the west end of the present Davenport Avenue—was to have been the point of crossing the river, but the Americans having torn up the bridge and planted two cannon there, General Garth found it necessary to march to the bridge at Hotchkisstown, now known as Westville. Meantime the Americans kept up a galling fire, which made the British march extremely hazardous. At the junction of the old West Haven road and the Milford turnpike one of their bravest officers, Adjutant Campbell, was killed. Finally, at about noon, the British succeeded, after renewed resistance from the citizens, in crossing into New Haven, and at about 1 o'clock reached the settled portion of the town, where they ransacked and pillaged many dwellings, burned storehouses and captured a number of prominent citizens. On the same day a party of British under General Tryon had landed at East Haven and captured Black Rock Fort, now Fort Hale (after a vigorous resistance from the nineteen Americans composing the garrison), but did not enter the town. The party under General Garth crossed to East Haven on Tuesday the 6th, and joined General Tryon, when, the militia having gathered in dangerously large numbers, the entire party of British went aboard their vessels and sailed away. The field-pieces which Captain Bradley and his men used in defending the pass on Whalley Avenue, on the day of the invasion, were located behind earthworks thrown up for the occasion. Traces of these earthworks were still visible fifty years after the close of the Revolutionary war.

WHALLEY AVENUE AND VICINITY—The Jewish cemetery lies on the north side of Whalley Avenue, opposite Hamilton Park (described elsewhere). The group of brick buildings seen at a distance of perhaps a third of a mile to the south of Whalley Avenue, from a point just east of Hamilton Park, constitutes the New Haven Alms-house, located at the head of Martin Street. Half a mile, perhaps, nearer the business part of the city, stands the New Haven County jail, an extensive brick structure on Whalley Avenue, at the corner of Hudson Street.

THE NEW HAVEN ORPHAN ASYLUM.—One block south of Whalley Avenue, at the corner of Elm and Beers streets, stands the New Haven Orphan Asylum, one of the largest and best managed of New Haven's many excellent institutions of charity. The asylum was organized in 1833, and since that time has afforded a home to more than twelve hundred children. The building at present used was built specially for the purpose in 1853, and a wing was added in 1864. On the first floor are the parlors, sitting-room, dining-room, kitchen and the sewing-room. On the next floor are the apartments of the mat-ron and teachers, the nursery, bath-rooms, etc., and on the third floor are the hospital and sleeping-rooms. The managers of the asylum are chosen from the different Protestant Evangelical religious denominations of the city.

OTHER POINTS OF INTEREST.—To the north of Whalley Avenue, where it intersects Sperry Street, is the quarter occupied by the colored population. In the district are several churches and a flourishing military company, managed entirely by colored people.

Continuing east on Whalley Avenue, the Gothic wooden church edifice at the junction of the avenue with Elm Street, is Christ Episco-pal Church.

York Square, a beautiful little park surrounded by houses of the Grecian style of architecture, lies twenty-five or thirty rods east of this point.

THE FIRE DEPARTMENT.—The brick structure, with tower attached, opposite Christ Church, is the house of Steam Fire Engine No. 3, one of the six steam fire-engine houses of the city of New Haven. There are also two hook-and-ladder houses, a supply house, etc., connected with the department, which is admirably managed, and has no superiors, of its size, in America. The number of men in the department is about 112, including a chief engineer, fire marshal, two assistant engineers and a superintendent of fire-alarm telegraph. Several permanent men are attached to each company. In the almost vital matter of good hose, New Haven probably takes the lead of every other city in the world.

From the southerly end of Whalley Avenue, it is but a short distance to High Street, on which, at the corner of Wall Street, is the :—

HOPKINS GRAMMAR SCHOOL.—In 1657, Governor Edward Hopkins, of Connecticut, died in London, leaving to trustees a bequest "for the breeding up of hopeful youths, both at the Grammar School and College, for the public service of the country in future times." Accordingly, in 1660 the school contemplated by the bequest was established in New Haven, about $2,000 having been realized from the bequest. The land was granted by the town. Ever since its establishment the Hopkins Grammar School has been maintained continuously, and is, perhaps, the oldest school continued without interruption, in America. It is certainly one of the best. The Hopkins Grammar School is chiefly a preparatory institution for the undergraduate departments of the University, and annually sends up a large class for admission. Its pupils are drawn from all parts of the world. The school, which is very fortunate in the possession of its present rector, Mr. W. L. Cushing, is under the supervision of a board of trustees, all of whom are officers or friends of Yale College.

THE NEW HAVEN CITY BURIAL GROUND.—The City Burial Ground, the entrance to which is through a great Egyptian gateway of sandstone, at the north end of High Street, on Grove Street, is a beautiful cemetery, laid out in the latter part of the last century, through the efforts of Mr. James Hillhouse and others. Within its limits have been buried the remains of many distinguished persons. Among the number were those whose names follow. The Paths (Hawthorn, Woodbine, Myrtle and Ivy) run approximately east and west, or perpendicular to High Street, while the Avenues (Sylvan, Cypress, Maple, Linden, Central, Magnolia, Laurel, Locust, Cedar, Spruce, Sycamore, Holly and Pine) run about north and south, parallel with the direction of High Street, Sylvan Avenue being on the east side of the cemetery, while the other avenues are located from that point in the order above mentioned, Pine Avenue being on the extreme west. T. indicates the tier, and N. the number of the lot in the tier, a tier being the land between two avenues. Tier Number 1 is in the east, the numbers increasing from east to west.

SYLVAN AVENUE.—Rev. Dr. Samuel W. S. Dutton, T. 1, N. 1.

CYPRESS AVENUE.—Henry Trowbridge, shipping merchant, T. 2, N. 42½; Professor James L. Kingsley, LL.D., T. 1, N. 45½.

MAPLE AVENUE.—Timothy Dwight, President Y. C., T. 3, N. 2; Jeremiah Day, President Y. C., T. 3, N. 34; James Hillhouse, LL.D., U. S. Senator 1794–1810, T. 2, N. 35; James A. Hillhouse, the poet of Sachem's Wood, T. 2, N. 37; A. N. Skinner, Mayor, teacher and tutor, T. 2, N. 67; Jonathan Ingersoll, Lieutenant-Governor, T. 2, N. 3; Hon. Ralph I. Ingersoll, T. 2, N. 3; David Daggett, LL.D., T. 2, N. 27; Simeon and Roger S. Baldwin, lawyers, T. 3, N. 30; Andrew H. Foote, Rear Admiral United States Navy, T. 3, N. 10; Augustus R. Street, great benefactor of Y. C., T. 3, N. 10; Nathan Smith, lawyer and United States Senator, T. 3, N. 58; Worthington Hooker, M.D., T. 2, N. 7; Henry W. Edwards, Governor, T. 3, N. 4; monument to Ezra Stiles, President Y. C., T. 3, N. 40.

LINDEN AVENUE.—Edward Herrick, librarian Y. C., T. 3, N. 25; Nathan Smith, M.D., T. 3, N. 1.

LOCUST AVENUE.—Amos B. Eaton, General, T. 8, N. 1; Eli Ives, M.D., T. 8, N. 25; Rev. Dr. Elisha S. Cleaveland, T. 8, N. 57; Rev. Dr. Harry Crosswell, editor, 1802–14, and rector of Trinity Church, 1815–38, T. 8, N. 17.

CEDAR AVENUE.—Colonel David Humphreys, aide of Washington, T. 9, N. 5; Rev. Lyman Beecher, D.D., "the most widely-known preacher in the country between

1815 and 1851," father of Rev. Henry Ward Beecher, T. 8. N. 20; Jedediah Morse, the father of American Geography, T. 8, N. 6; Rev. Dr. Nathaniel W. Taylor, T. 8, N. 20; Benjamin Silliman, Professor of Chemistry in Y. C. 1802–55, one of the foremost scientists of his time, T. 8, N. 4; Rev. Samuel Merwin, T. 8, N. 18; Noah Webster, author of the standard dictionary of the English language, and of " Webster's Spelling Book," which had a sale of 50,000,000 copies, T. 8, N. 24; Eli Whitney, inventor of the cotton-gin, T. 8, N. 22; Major Theodore Winthrop, A.M., T. 8, N. 14; Jonathan Knight, M.D., T. 9, N. 29; Denison Olmsted, Professor of Natural Philosophy and Astronomy in Y. C., 1825–59; James Brewster, T. 9, N. 51; C. A. Goodrich, Professor of Rhetoric in Y. C., 1817–39.

SPRUCE AVENUE.—Admiral Francis H. Gregory.

HAWTHORN PATH.—Jehudi Ashmun, first colonial agent at Liberia, T. 5, N. 54.

THE FIRST METHODIST CHURCH.—The church edifice a few blocks distant from the City Burial Ground, on the northeast corner of Elm and College streets, diagonally opposite Battell Chapel, is that belonging to the First Methodist Episcopal Society, which was organized in 1795, and first met in a building on Gregson Street. The present edifice was built in 1849, $75,000 having been appropriated by the town to the society on the condition that the latter should give up its site on the Green.

THE OLD STATE HOUSE.—The Grecian building on the western side of the Green, near College Street, is known as the Old State House. It was built by the State about half a century ago, and until within a few years was the semi-capitol of Connecticut. It also served for some time in the capacity of a court-house, and has recently been put to other uses. Three of its rooms, numbers 2, 3 and 4, are occupied by the New Haven Colony Historical Society, an organization founded in 1862 by a number of New Haven gentlemen interested in preserving the history and relics connected with the New Haven Colony. For many years the society kept its collection in a room in the City Hall, but in January, 1881, moved into its present quarters, in the Old State House. The rooms of the society will well repay a visit, and strangers can obtain admission on any day from 10 A.M. to 5 P.M.

The collection of relics is very complete and interesting. The table on which Noah Webster wrote his dictionary; Benedict Arnold's sign, medicine chest, mortar and pestle and account book, and a Leyden jar once the property of Benjamin Franklin, may be mentioned as objects which are of interest to every one. Many fine portraits of old New Haven citizens cover the walls of the library, while a number of historic engravings, and photographs of houses famous in by-gone days are to be seen in a room devoted exclusively to relics of old New Haven. The library is small, though well selected and very valuable, the collection of pamphlets being very complete. No one visiting New Haven should leave the city without seeing the rooms of the society and carefully examining its collections.

With the Old State House the tour of the western portion of New Haven, and in fact of the city, comes to a close. In a work so brief, it has been impossible to give more than a passing glance at many objects and places worthy of much attention. For want of space, too, numerous articles which would otherwise have occupied a place in the work have been omitted. It is hoped, however, that the visitor has been shown a great majority of the more important objects of interest in and about New Haven, and that he has been able to obtain a fair idea of the "City of Elms."

"Peace be within thy Walls, O Yale, and Prosperity within thy Palaces! May Erudition, Religion and every Virtue be the ornament of thy Sons! May thy Renown and Glory be diffused through the Republic of Letters, and be Commensurate with the Expansion of Science and Knowledge, and with the Duration and Liberty of these United States."